THE DAY THAT ELVIS CAME TO TOWN

Other Avon Camelot Books by
Jan Marino

EIGHTY-EIGHT STEPS TO SEPTEMBER

JAN MARINO has written three books for young people including *Eighty-Eight Steps to September* and is at work on her next book.

She lives in Oyster Bay, New York, with her husband.

THE DAY THAT ELVIS CAME TO TOWN

JAN MARINO

For Len

AVON BOOKS
A division of
The Hearst Corporation
1350 Avenue of the Americas
New York, New York 10019

Published by arrangement with Little, Brown and Company, Inc.
Library of Congress Catalog Card Number: 90-13493
ISBN: 0-380-71672-0
RL: 5.0

First Avon Camelot Printing: February 1993

Printed in the U.S.A.

OPM 10 9 8 7 6 5 4 3 2 1

THE DAY THAT ELVIS CAME TO TOWN

Chapter 1

"Better clean up that bathroom real good, Wanda," my mother called up the stairs. "We've got a new boarder for the room in the attic. She's coming in on the noon bus."

"I thought you said once April May moved out of the attic, I could have my room back."

"Be patient, Wanda. Be patient."

Another boarder. That meant I'd never get my room back. Or any room, for that matter. There'd always be another April May, or somebody, to take up the extra space.

"How's it coming, Wanda?" she called again. "It'll be noon before you know it."

"I'm going as fast as I can," I shouted.

Ever since I was twelve or so, we'd had boarders sleeping all over our house. First one to move in was my aunt. "Where'd you expect me to go, Augie?" she'd said to my father. "I've got nobody in Claxton now that Momma's gone."

My father grumbled something about it being all right and that she was welcome, but when she wasn't around he'd say things like "It was a pretty sorry day the day I opened my front door and found April May standing there, bag and baggage, but it got sorrier when I told her she could come on in." Or "You can pick your friends, but the good Lord doesn't give you a choice when it comes to your relatives."

My mother never did like April May. "She's just like your mother," she'd say to my father. And my mother certainly didn't like my father's mother. "I cannot understand what kind of a woman would name her children after their birth month," she'd say. And when I'd asked her why April May was named after two months, she told me April May was slow even then. "She took her time and didn't arrive fully until ten minutes after twelve on May first."

"Is it ready, Wanda?" my mother called. "I want to put fresh towels in there."

"It's done," I said.

I hated cleaning up bathrooms after other people. It was bad enough that April May took sponge baths every day and left puddles all over the place, but it was worse when she took a bath. She was so fat she couldn't make it out of the tub on her own, so I'd have to stop whatever I was doing to haul her on out. "You'll see, Miss Twiggy," she'd say. "You'll get there. We all add a few pounds every year."

And I hated all the other work, too. Like bringing the boarders fresh linen every week. April May would stand in her doorway and make a fuss if I didn't bring hers first. "Seems like you've got your favorites," she'd say. "Always bringing me the mended stuff. Always taking the best sheets to Calvin and Mr. Gingrich. Always putting me last."

"That's not so, April May," Mr. Collins would call out from his room. "Wanda is a fair young lady. As fair as the day is long. Wanda, in the words of Cicero, gives everyone his due."

April May would call out for Mr. Collins and Cicero to shut up and then she'd slam her door.

And then there was Mr. Gingrich. He'd take about two hours to thank me for bringing him his linen, telling me how much he appreciated the smell of fresh sheets, telling me how much they reminded him of his momma, telling me how good it was to have such a fine landlady, telling me how good it was to live in such a fine house —

"Wanda," my mother called, "I'm on my way."

I took one last swipe at the floor, spritzed the mirror, rubbed it dry, and then put everything under the sink for the next time.

"Make sure you marry a man who can keep a few dollars in his pocket," my mother said as she came up the stairs, towels stacked up from her arms to her chin. "Don't let anybody tell you money doesn't help. Believe me, it helps."

My mother was always saying things like that. She resented having to take people in so that we could stay in our house. She loved the house; at least she had before the boarders came. It was almost like it was alive to her. She used to say things like "Isn't the living room friendly?" And when she walked into the kitchen, she used to say, "I love this kitchen. It's always smiling." But she hadn't said that lately.

Now she said things like "Life surely doesn't go in a straight path, does it." Then she would close her eyes, rub her back, and sigh. "But things will be better once your father digs himself out of the hole he's gotten himself into."

I didn't want my life to be like that. I didn't want to be like my mother, staying in Harmony all my life. She always told me how much she had wanted to go away to college but her father wouldn't hear of it. So she commuted to the state college to become a teacher. That's where she met my father. They fell in love and got married before they graduated. And then they had me.

"Wanda," I heard my mother say, "your mind is wandering again. I've asked you at least three times to get the puff down from the top shelf."

I pulled the puff down, handed it to my mother, and walked down the hall, through my parents' bedroom and into the sun porch where I slept. I closed the door behind me. I hated sleeping in that room. I didn't mind all the windows. I liked the sun that streamed in, and I didn't mind the streetlights that shone in at night. What I hated was the glass door leading to my parents' room. My father had put a shade on it, but even with the shade down, I felt like I was in a glass bubble. A big glass bubble.

I put my record player on and waited for the music

to start, and when it did, I kept time and sang along with Elvis. "*. . . they been so long on lonely street they ain't never gonna come back . . .*"

— *I wonder if this will be the last boarder. Mr. Collins was supposed to be the very last, but he wasn't.*

I held up my hands, closed my eyes, and danced, pretending Elvis was holding me. "*. . . I get so lonely, I could die . . .*"

— *I hope Poppa's all right. He was fidgety this morning. Then Momma started on him.*

"Wanda," I heard my mother call.

— *Someday I'm going to have a place where no one can find me.*

"Wanda," she called again. Loud.

— *I wish I had that place now.*

"Wanda." Louder.

I stopped dancing.

— *"Thank you for the dance,"* I whispered.

"Do. You. Hear. Me?"

"I hear you," I called back.

"Then come down and help the new boarder up with her bags."

I lifted my record from the phonograph, slipped it into its jacket, and started downstairs.

"I don't cook meals, Miss Washington," I could hear my mother say as I came down the stairs. "I do allow some of the boarders to use the kitchen, for cooking only, but that would be an extra two dollars a week. And to tell you the truth, I don't encourage it. I like my kitchen more or less to myself."

"Oh, I don't think I'll be using it much. Maybe for a cup of coffee . . ."

"Well, then, that will be only a dollar a week," my mother said. "Wanda," she said when she saw me, "this is Miss MER-ce-dees Washington . . ."

"Mer-SAY-dees, Mrs. Dohr. My name is pronounced with the accent on the *say*."

"Oh," my mother said. "Wanda, this is Mer-SAY-dees Washington. Miss Washington, this is my daughter Wanda."

She smiled at me. Her teeth were small white Chiclets. There were four suitcases at her feet. They were covered with stickers from different places. She had tanned skin, the color of homemade coffee ice cream with lots and lots of cream in it. Her eyes were big and soft and green. Her hair was almost black, and it curled around her face the way I wanted mine to do. She was beautiful. She was the most beautiful person I'd ever seen.

"Miss Washington," my mother said, "Wanda will help you up with your bags."

"Mercedes," she said. "Please call me Mercedes." Then she looked over at me. "You, too, Wanda. Mercedes. That's my name."

And for the first time since the boarders came, I felt like something good was going to happen.

Chapter 2

I reached for the two large bags, but she put her hand out and said, "Sweetie, Mercedes Washington is used to toting her own belongings. But if you'd care to help me with those two small bags, I'd be much obliged."

I smiled at her and picked up the small cases. They were so heavy I nearly fell over.

"Makeup," she said, starting up the stairs.

"Makeup?" I said. She looked like she didn't use one drop of anything.

"Stage makeup, honey. Nothing but stage makeup."

And before I could ask her what kind of stage she was talking about, my mother was calling up to her for her to feel free to come down to fix herself a cup of tea or a cup of coffee, and Mercedes was calling back a kindly thank-you, and April May was calling to me from her room to bring her a glass of iced ginger tea on my next trip upstairs, and Mr. Collins was calling out to April May to be quiet.

"Your momma said my room is in the attic. That right, hon?"

I nodded. "It used to be my room," I said. "That is, until my aunt came."

"Where's your aunt now?" she said, resting her bags on the landing.

I motioned toward April May's room with my head and said, "April May told Momma she was going to have an asthma attack going up all those stairs, so Momma put her in one of the second-floor bedrooms."

"So how come you never got your room back?"

"Momma says we need the money."

"Oh," she said, and she started climbing again.

When we got to the attic, I handed her the key and she opened the door. "Well," she said, plunking down her bags and walking in the room and smiling and turning around all at the same time, "isn't this something." She went over to the alcove and stood by the window. The curtains blew in and wrapped themselves around her. She laughed and pushed them away. "This is like something out of a fairy tale. The one where the girl lets her hair down and her lover climbs up and takes her away."

"Rapunzel," I said.

"Yeah," she said softly. "Rapunzel. She let down her hair and went off and lived happily ever after."

Then she went over to the bed, which was under the lowest part of the eaves. Her hands rubbed the small blue and white pattern of the wallpaper, and then she smoothed the quilt my mother had made for my bed. She looked down at the braided rug and smiled, and when she saw the old wicker rocking chair in the corner, she said, "This is the prettiest place I've ever stayed. Oh, I've been to plenty of places. Big city hotels with fancy rooms, but never anything like this. This is sweet. Real sweet. It'll be good leaving the city behind and coming home to this. Especially after a long gig."

"A gig?" I said. "What's a gig?"

"You don't know what a gig is, sweetie?" And before I could answer her, she said, "A gig is a job. I'm a singer."

"You mean you sing for a living?" I said, thinking about all the ladies down at church who sang.

"I sure do, but it's not easy." She began to sing, "I get a gig here, get a gig there, here a gig, there a gig, everywhere a gig, gig. Old Mercedes gets those gigs, yessirree she does."

Then she flopped down on the bed, stretched her arms over her head, and said, "Wanda, honey, I'm loving this place already." She looked over at me and said, "You come and visit anytime, hon. Anytime."

I thanked her and started toward the door. "Hey," she called, "how'd you like to help me unpack? I got an extra dollar or two in my pocket that's not doing anything."

"Sure," I said, "but I don't want anything."

"Honey, you don't do nothing for nothing." Then

she got up and swung one of the suitcases onto the bed and started to unpack. She had more dresses than I'd ever seen before. Even in Fenton's Department Store. "Stage clothes," she said. "You got to look good when you're up there."

She took them out one at a time, shook them, smoothed them, and hung them in the closet. Some had feathers and some were nothing but sequins and beads. "Makes me sparkle on stage, hon. That's what you got to do. Sparkle."

"They're beautiful," I said. "I've never seen dresses this beautiful."

She reached in and took out a sky-blue gown. The sleeves were long and puffed and there was a bow at the neck. "Here," she said, "try it on, sweetie. It matches your eyes."

I shook my head.

"Go on," she said. "It's yours. I've worn this dress so many times, it doesn't owe me a thing. Go ahead." And she pushed it into my arms.

I went into the alcove and slipped out of my dress and into hers. It felt strange, like nothing I'd ever had on before. Soft. And it smelled so sweet. Just like Mercedes. The whole room smelled like Mercedes.

I smoothed my hands over the silky skirt. I ran my hands down the arms. I rubbed my cheek into my shoulder. Then I tied the bow.

"Come on out from behind there and show me what you look like," she said. And when I came out from the alcove, she smiled at me and said, "You're sparkling. Just sparkling."

I turned around and looked at myself in the mirror.

"You know what you need, hon?" And before I answered, she said, "A little color. Just a little or your momma might show me the door." Then she opened one of the makeup cases and began to make me up. When she was finished, she stood back and said, "Why, sweetie, you're real pretty. Now take a look at yourself." And she handed me a mirror.

I did look pretty. I even felt pretty, sitting there in my old room with Mercedes fussing over me. I even felt happy. I looked up at her and smiled and said, "Thank you. Thanks a lot."

"For nothing," she said. "Come on, let's get this stuff away. I've been traveling since five o'clock this morning and I am one tired lady."

We emptied both bags and when we were finished she put a feathered hat on her head and a sequin band on mine. Then she took my hands and started to dance. After a few steps, she laughed and said, "Well, I know what we can work on next." She threw the feathered hat in the corner and collapsed on the bed. "Hon," she said, "I'm going to take me a little nap." Then she reached into her pocket and handed me two dollars.

"No," I said. "You gave me the dress and I enjoyed doing it. It was fun."

"Fun or not, sweetie, you take this," she said, pressing the money into my hand. "Remember what I said.

You don't do nothing for nothing." Then she lay back and looked around the room. She closed her eyes for a minute. When she opened them she looked around one more time and said, "Well, I'm sure glad I didn't dream all of this." Then she smiled at me, smoothed the quilt, and shut her eyes.

I closed the door quietly behind me and went down to the kitchen. My mother was standing at the sink, her back to me, and when she heard me she said, "What in the world were you doing up there? April May's been fussing about that fool ginger tea."

"Oh, Momma," I said, "you have to see Mercedes's clothes. They're beautiful. She's a singer and she's been everywhere. She's got all those stickers on her bags. She's been to big cities all over. Oh, Momma, I had such a good time."

"That's nice, Wanda," she said, "but I don't want your head getting filled with highfalutin ideas." Then she turned to me and her eyes opened wide. "Wanda Sue Dohr, what do you have on your face? And what is that you've got on?"

"Isn't it beautiful?" I said, putting my own dress on the kitchen chair and twirling around so that the skirt swished around the floor. "Mercedes gave it to me. And she just put a little makeup on me for fun. That's all."

"Well, you just go wash it off before anybody sees you like that. And don't start imagining things, like how glamorous it'd be to be on the stage."

"Momma!"

"Don't 'Momma' me. And for heaven's sake get out of that dress before you fall and kill yourself." Then she walked over to me and felt the material in the skirt and said, "This is a fine piece of fabric. Real fine."

"Oh, Momma, you should see her other dresses and you —"

But before I could finish, the radiator banged. Momma dropped the material, rubbed her hands on her apron, and said, "There she goes again. Take her tea up, will you? I don't much feel like having her visiting in my kitchen."

I stuck my dress under my arm, took April May's tea from my mother, and started up the stairs. April May was sitting in the chair by the window. She always sat there. She'd watch everybody go by and call to them a sweet hello and then say something nasty about them under her breath. Then Petey, her parakeet, would call out, "Hello. Hello," until April May shook his cage and told him to be quiet. I hated it when she did that. Petey was a sweet little thing. He was all white except for his eyes. They were red. "A freak of nature," April May called him. She always told Petey he was a lucky bird and that nobody else wanted him. But my father said that wasn't true and that Petey was special.

"You look like a little tart in that dress," she said when I handed her the tea. "And what's that on your face?"

I didn't answer. But that didn't stop her. She went

on to say, "What kind of a name is Mercedes?" And to say that she'd seen Mercedes going on up to her room and that the stickers on her bags were more than likely phony ones, and that she probably was a big phony, too. But I didn't care.

"Watcha doin'? Watcha doin'?" Petey said, flapping his wings against the cage. That's about the only other thing Petey ever said.

"You're supposed to say good-bye, Petey. Good-bye when somebody leaves you," I called back. Then I walked down the hall, through my parents' room and into mine. I pulled down the shade and put Elvis back on my record player. Then I closed my eyes and kept time to the music.

— *I hope Mercedes stays forever. I don't even mind that she's in my room, because when I was there with her, it almost seemed like my room again.*

I sang along with Elvis. Softly.

— *Poppa would like her, too. Maybe we'll all go to see her at her gigs.*

I put my hand in Elvis's and started to dance.

— *I'm pretty,* I whispered. *Poppa says so. And Mercedes does, too.*

"Wanda. Wanda Sue," my mother called from outside my door. "It's time to set the table for supper. And I'll need you to go down to the market for a loaf of bread. And make sure you tell April May to bring her tea glass down. The last time she left it under the bed, and you know what that brought in the house. A whole mess of roaches."

I stopped dancing, took my record from the phonograph, and put it back into its jacket. Then I slipped out of Mercedes's dress and back into my own.

"I'm coming, Momma," I said. And then I whispered, "I'll be back. I promise."

Chapter 3

"April May, take your tea glass down to the kitchen when you come down," I called. "My mother said."

"Your mother says. Your mother says," she mimicked. "If it ain't your mother saying, it's your father saying. Or you saying. It'll be a happy day when Murph takes me away from all this."

"Watcha doin'? Watcha doin'?"

"Where's he taking you, April May?" I asked, but she didn't hear me.

Murph was the Mr. Murphy who used to live up in my room. My mother had, in her words, turned him out one fine day. I never knew the exact cause, but I did hear my father say to my mother, "Why, Jane Ann, he was just doing what comes natural for a fellow."

"You call a fifty-three-year-old a fellow?" my mother had said. "I call him a dirty old man."

But even though Mr. Murphy had been turned out, it wasn't the end of him. He came to call for April May in his car every chance he had. My mother said it was more like a small house than a car. "It's a classic," my father would say. "One day it's going to be a collector's item. Be worth something."

"The day that Mr. Murphy has two nickels to buy a gallon of gas, let alone a lot of money, will be a day I'll never live to see," my mother would say.

It was true. They never went anywhere. They'd just sit in the car. Sometimes April May would pack a picnic lunch and when it was time to eat, Mr. Murphy would spread a blanket out on the lawn. He'd take April May's hand and help her onto the blanket, and then he'd sit beside her and gaze at her as if she were a movie star.

"Look at them," my mother would say, peering out of the parlor window. "For the life of me, I cannot understand how anybody could go out with a man who fashions his front teeth out of candle wax. Even April May."

"Where's Mr. Murphy going to take you, April May?" I called out again.

"Anywhere," she called back. "Anywhere but here."

"Be it ever so humble, there's no place like home," Mr. Collins called out from his room. "You just think about those words, April May. There's a considerable amount of wisdom in those words."

"Oh, shut up, Calvin," April May said, slamming her door.

"Watcha doin'? Watcha doin'?" I could hear Petey call.

"Anger is momentary madness, so control your passion, April May, or it will control you," Mr. Collins said. "Horace said that."

Mr. Collins didn't talk like other people. He was always quoting somebody or other or making up quotations of his own. My mother liked it. "Mr. Collins gives this place class," she'd say. "And the Lord knows we can use it."

She didn't feel that way about the rest of the boarders. But it was her own fault. I swear — and I told her one day — that when there's an empty room and she puts an ad in the paper, she must write: "Send me your poor, your strange, your nutty ones," because that's just what comes on by when there's a room to rent.

All except Mercedes. She was different.

I went into the kitchen and took twenty-five cents from the sugar bowl. "Are you sure that's all you need? Just bread?"

"Just bread, Wanda." But before I got myself out the door, she called, "Wanda. Wanda Sue. You want to do your momma a big favor?"

And before she got the words out of her mouth, I knew what she was going to say.

"What?" I said, sighing a big sigh.

"Stop by the store and walk home with Poppa. Today's the fifteenth of the month, and you know what that is."

I knew what the fifteenth was. It was the day most of Poppa's customers paid him. I wanted to close my ears and pretend I didn't hear her. I hated it when she did this.

"Now, Wanda," she said, smoothing my hair, "just pretend you were walking on by. After you pick up the bread, that is. Just walk on by. Okay, Wanda? That okay with you?"

"Yes," I said. "It's okay with me."

But what I really wanted to say was it wasn't okay with me, and why didn't she do it instead of her staying home all the time? Having me walk on by as though he didn't know what I was doing. But he knew. He'd pretend it was a good idea, but he knew what I was up to. I hated to do it, but I was always doing it anyway because I was always afraid Poppa would go to MacPherson's Tavern and start up again.

"Don't forget now, Wanda. Just pretend you were walking on by."

I went down the walk and tried to think about other things. I thought about Mercedes and what a good time I'd had this afternoon. I wondered what she was doing up in my room. Was she still sleeping? Was she getting ready to go to a gig? Then I remembered she told me I could stop by and visit anytime. I decided that when I got home I was going to do just that. Maybe I could get Momma to ask her down for supper. Usually my mother didn't invite the boarders down. Except for one Sunday a month. She'd fix a big dinner with turkey and sweet potatoes and pies. She'd set the dining room table with her finest lace cloth and cloth napkins. After dinner, she'd ask Mr. Collins to do some reciting. The boarders never seemed to mind when they found a seventy-five-cent charge on their month's rent.

"Hey there, Wanda Sue," Gerard Flitty said when I got to Flitty's Convenience Store. "That's a pretty hair ribbon you've got on."

Gerard's uncle owned Flitty's, and Gerard worked there after school and all summer. He was always trying to walk home with me. Sarah, my best friend, told me he was trying to do more than walk me home. "He's trying to get into your skirts."

"What would he want to do that for?" I'd said. And when she told me, I never was able to look Gerard in his little round pig eyes again.

I looked down at my shoes, thanked him for the compliment, paid him for the bread, and started down to get Poppa. Seeing Gerard made me think of Sarah. I missed her. Every summer her family went away, and this summer they were in California for over two months. We never went anywhere. Poppa was always promising to take us away but it never seemed to happen. "Someday," he'd say. "Someday we're going to take the Grand Tour."

When I got to Poppa's shop, I knew I was too late. All the lights were out except the one in the back. I could see Mr. Gingrich putting away some tools. Then he took his hat from the shelf, put it on, and came out. "Well, hello, Wanda. Isn't this a nice surprise. I was just thinking how nice it'd be if you stopped on by . . ."

"Is Poppa here?" I asked.

He started to talk about how good it was to see me and how business had seen better days and how sad it was that a lot of the customers were dying off. "That's what happens. New folks just don't take care of their plumbing problems like the old folks did."

"Is Poppa here?" I asked again. "I was just walking by and I thought I could walk home with him."

Mr. Gingrich shrugged and said, "Think he might have started home a little early. But I'll be happy to walk with you."

He shut out the last light, put the Closed for the Day sign in the window, locked the door, and we started home. Mr. Gingrich had one of his one-way conversations all the way home. I was glad, because I was busy praying. Praying that when we got home, Poppa would be there and everything would be okay. Praying supper would be on the table and the knot in my stomach would leave.

"You should have walked faster," my mother said when I put the bread on the table. "Now look what he's gone and done." She stopped peeling the carrots and sighed.

"He's never done it before, Momma?" I said. "Like it's my fault because I didn't get there fast enough and Poppa wasn't there." I could feel the tears starting up.

She got up quickly and came over to me. "I'm sorry, Wanda. I'm really sorry. It's just that it's getting to me more and more every time he does it. I don't know. I just don't know."

She walked over to the stove and began to stir whatever she had in the pot. "It's getting harder," she said to nobody in particular. Then she turned to me and asked me to take April May's tray upstairs. "She never brought her tea glass down. Bring it down for me, Wanda. Please."

"Sure, Momma," I said, taking the tray in my hands.

Supper was the only meal that Momma wouldn't stand for April May eating with us. "It's the only time of the day we have together," she'd say. My father felt the same way, but when he was "in his cups," as Momma called it, he'd say, "You know, Jane Ann, April May is my sister and blood is thicker than water." To which my mother would reply, "So is mud."

"Well, it's about time," April May said when I came into her room. "A body could flop with hunger around here. It ain't my fault your mother wants me to eat in my room all by myself. Nothing to do but look out the window."

"Watcha doin'? Watcha doin'?"

I took a piece of corn bread from April May's tray and went over to Petey's cage. "Here, Petey boy. Come on, come and get it."

Petey hopped from his perch and came to the side of the cage.

"Don't you let him out."

"I won't," I said, putting my finger into the cage to smooth Petey's feathers.

The only time April May let Petey out of his cage was when she cleaned it. Then she'd put him in a shoe box she'd poked holes in. One day I asked her why she never let him fly around. "'Cause he's mine," she'd said. And then she told me to mind my own business.

Petey took the bread from my hand and flew back to his perch. "See you later, Petey," I said.

"Hello. Hello."

My mother and I ate our dinner in silence, and when we were finished, I cleared off the table and said, "I think I'll go on up and visit with Mercedes for a while."

"She's not up there," my mother said. "Said she was going out for a bite to eat. You remember your place, now. She's a paying boarder and I don't want you to think you can go on up just any old time. Besides, I told you I didn't want you getting fancy ideas in your head."

"Momma, I like her. And she likes me."

"Why, you hardly know her."

"I do, Momma."

"How can you? She just came into this house this afternoon."

"I don't know. But I do."

My mother sighed and kind of shook her head.

The kitchen was beginning to fade. The light from outside got dimmer and dimmer. I could almost hear my own breath, it was so quiet. My mother just sat at the table, rubbing the tablecloth as though it would make my father appear.

"Wanda, honey," she said after a while, "why don't you go on up and do some reading or something? I'll just sit here awhile and wait for Poppa. He should be home soon."

But we both knew that wasn't going to happen.

When my father "broke out," as my mother sometimes said, he didn't come right home.

I kissed her and went up to my room.

I took out Elvis and put him on. His voice filled the room. I lay on my bed and stared up at the ceiling.

— *I hope Poppa's all right. I hate this. I hope he comes home before it gets real dark.*

I could hear April May arguing about something with Mr. Collins.

— *Someday there'll be just us. I'll have my own room again and I'll play Elvis as loud as I want. I'll dance, too. And Poppa can . . . God, please, please don't let him stay away too long . . .*

"Wanda. Wanda," I heard my mother call from the hall.

— *There she goes again. What does she want now?*

Then I realized it was Mercedes calling me. I put Elvis back into his cover, smoothed my hair, and went out to the hall.

She was standing at the top of the hall stairs wearing a pretty white dress with a pink silky scarf around her waist. She held out a paper bag and said, "Hi, there, sweetie. Guess what? I bought us some cherry ice cream down at the drugstore. Even got us some spoons. We can eat it out of the cartons."

I thanked her and we started up the stairs to the attic. "I brought some for your momma and poppa, too. She said she wasn't hungry so she put it in the fridge for later." Mercedes opened the door to her room. I sat on the floor and she settled herself in the rocker. "I'm going to be one busy lady," she said, scooping up some ice cream. "I'm booked into an old haunt of mine in Savannah. Two shows a night. Why, I'm going to see myself coming and going."

I took a huge spoonful filled with cherries. "Have you been to a lot of places?"

"I've been to so many places I don't remember half of them."

"My friend Sarah has gone somewhere every single summer since she was nine. I've never even been to Savannah."

"Maybe you can come to hear me sing some night."

"You mean it?"

"Sure," she said. "I'd like that."

When we were finished with the ice cream, Mercedes told me she once sang at a club in London. I asked her if she met the Queen, but she laughed and said she didn't keep that kind of company.

"But have you ever met anybody famous?"

"Why, sweetie, that's like asking Satchmo if he's got a horn."

"Who's that?"

"Why, that's Louis. Old Louis Armstrong, greatest trumpet player ever was. You never heard of him?"

I shook my head. "Who else do you know?"

But before she could answer me, there was such a commotion going on downstairs that Mercedes said, "Better get on down, hon. I think I hear your momma calling."

Chapter 4

Every light in the house was on and voices were coming from everywhere.

"Whatever do you mean, Mr. Gingrich?" my mother was saying. "Why would August go up to New York? He's never been farther than Charlottesville."

"Calm down, Miz Dohr. I never said it was a certainty that Augie went to New York. I just said there was a strong possibility."

"Oh, dear God," Momma said. Then she began to wail and walk around and around the upstairs hall. She looked like Petey trying to get out of his cage.

Then she stopped and turned to Mr. Gingrich and said in almost a holler, "What makes you think August has taken off for New York?"

"Miz Dohr," Mr. Gingrich said, "if you'll calm down a mite, I'll commence to tell you."

My mother sat down on the stairs, put her head on her knees, and rocked back and forth, moaning over and over, "Oh, dear God, what's next?"

Mr. Gingrich stood over her. "This morning, as is his wont every morning, Augie went down to the post office to pick up the mail. I think it was around ten, or maybe it was closer to ten-thirty because Miz Plum, Miz Charley Plum, that is, called to complain about the job we did for her back in April and that was 'long about ten-thirty . . ."

"Please, Mr. Gingrich," my mother said, her voice slightly less loud than a holler. "What did August say?"

"Well, as I was saying, Augie went on down for the mail like he does every morning and when he came on back, he proceeded to call me out from the back room. Nothing unusual about Augie's doing that. Does it all the time . . ."

"Please, Mr. Gingrich," Momma said again, a holler coming through her teeth.

"Well, seems that Augie found some kind of adver*tise*ment that said every plumber in the entire United States owed it to his customers to go on to the American, or maybe it was the All-American . . ."

April May came out of her room, carrying Petey's cage. "Get on with it," April May said. "A body'd think you were reporting to the FBI, having to get every fool detail into all of this."

"Yes," Mr. Gingrich said, "it was the All-American Plumbing Convention. The *All* was all done up in big red letters: A-L-L. I can see it now . . ."

"What'd he say?" April May said.

"Watcha doin'? Watcha doin'?"

". . . well, anyway, Augie said, 'George Gingrich' —

when Augie's making a serious point he always calls me by my full name — 'George Gingrich,' he said, 'I think that'd be a fine thing to do. Yes, sir, a very fine thing to do.' And then he walked out the door."

"Oh, Lord," my mother said. "Why would he want to go and do a thing like that? He didn't have anything with him. Not even an extra set of underwear."

"Don't worry about that," April May said. "I hear tell New York has some pretty big department stores. Bigger than Fenton's."

The knot in my stomach got bigger. "Oh, Poppa," I whispered, "come home."

"Hello. Hello. Hello . . ."

"Keep that bird quiet," my mother said.

"Can't say I blame my poor brother taking off like this," April May said. "Having to put up with the likes of some people I know."

"Hush up, April May," Mr. Collins said as he came out of his room and into the hallway. "You talk too much."

"You hush up."

"Oh, God," Momma said. "He's got the month's receipts with him."

"That all you can think about?" April May said. "The month's receipts. And him up in the wilds of New York. My only brother could be stretched out in an alley somewhere, his throat slit open, his eyes shut forever . . ."

"Watcha doin'? Watcha doin'?"

"April May," Mr. Collins said, "mind your bird and

your mouth. That is ugly talk you're talking. And those who have few things to attend to are great babblers, for the less they think, the more they talk."

"Who said that one, Calvin? Ben Franklin or Will what's his name?" April May said, slamming her door.

The knot in my stomach tightened, and I got to feeling so sick that I ran into the bathroom and threw up. But the knot stayed. In the mirror, my face was pale and sweaty. "Why, Poppa? Why did you do it?" I washed up quickly and went back to Momma.

"Excuse me," Mercedes said as she came down the attic stairs, "I don't mean to eavesdrop, but I've never heard such a flap about anything. Just 'cause a man decided to fly himself up to a convention. Why, he'll be home before you know it."

My mother looked up at Mercedes, her eyes flooded with tears, her face all red. I thought Momma would tell her she was eavesdropping and that she didn't belong here, but she didn't. "I wish I could believe that," she said. "I really do. But him doing something like this. He's probably in his cups."

"His what?"

"You know," my mother said.

"Drunk?"

My mother turned away.

"Well, hon, the worst thing that can happen is that he'll lose all the money he's got. And the best thing that can happen is that he'll get to the All-American Plumbing Convention and have himself one good time."

Momma began to cry again. Softly, though.

"Come on, Miz Dohr," Mercedes said. "It isn't the end of the world."

My mother kept crying and everything got crazy. April May opened her door. Petey called out "Watcha doin'? Watcha doin'? " about a million times. Mr. Gingrich introduced himself to Mercedes and told her how pleased he was to meet her. Mr. Collins bowed and said it was his pleasure, too. My mother told April May to make Petey stop. And then she cried louder.

"Crying won't bring him back any faster," Mercedes said.

Mr. Gingrich just stood looking at my mother, shaking his head back and forth. And Mr. Collins looked at Mercedes and said, "Well, now, somebody is using some good old common sense. And you know what old Horace Greeley once said . . ."

"No, we don't know what old Horace Greeley once said," April May said. "And we don't much care."

". . . common sense is very uncommon."

"'Specially in this house," Mr. Gingrich said in a voice barely above a whisper. Then he excused himself and went to his room.

"Come on, Miz Dohr," Mercedes said, "I'll fix you a nice hot cup of tea and you'll feel a lot better. Promise you."

Momma didn't move.

Mercedes reached down and took my mother's arm and helped her up. "I'll just bet he'll be calling you in about an hour or so. It takes a while to get up there —"

My mother let out a big sob and took in a deep breath.

"— even by plane."

And then, as if my mother were a little girl, Mercedes took her hand and led her down into the kitchen. She brewed a pot of tea and just as she began to pour, April May's radiator banged.

"What's that?" Mercedes asked.

"April May," I said.

"What in the world does she want now?" my mother said.

She banged again.

"Better go on up, Wanda. She doesn't give up easy," my mother said.

I started to get up, but Mercedes took my arm and said, "Have your tea first." Then, quickly looking over at Momma, she said, "Sorry, Miz Dohr, I've got to learn to mind my own business."

I waited for my mother to say Mercedes *should* mind her own business. But she didn't. She sighed, shrugged, and said, "She's right. Have your tea first. April May will be there and be there and be there."

Mercedes laughed and said, "That was well put."

Momma began to rub the kitchen table. Her hand went round and round and round. Then the tears started up again. "He's a good man, Miss Washington . . ."

"Mercedes, please."

". . . Mercedes. A good man. But he gets these spells . . ."

"Drinking," Mercedes said. "It's the drink."

"Then he forgets he's got a home to come home to."

"I know," Mercedes said, softly. "I know."

I never saw anybody as tender with someone as Mercedes was with my mother. Mercedes sat with her and rubbed her hand and smoothed her hair. She fixed Momma more tea and made some cinnamon toast and when April May started to bang on the radiator again, Mercedes just poured us more tea.

When my mother finished, Mercedes cleared up and told her to go on up to bed. "He'll call you soon. And I'll just bet he'll be home before morning."

Mercedes was wrong. I stayed awake until the last street lamp went off. But when I heard the garbage truck coming down the street, I knew he wouldn't be coming home.

He didn't come home till three nights later. He came in the house as though nothing had happened. Like he'd never been away. Carrying a huge teddy bear. Singing his favorite song. Only he'd made up new words.

"Wanda Dohr. Wanda Dohr.
No one else could ask for more.
Like the heather on the moor, and the sands upon the shore.
Wanda Dohr. Wanda Dohr.
Like a shining light you are.
Never go very far
From your father, Wanda Dohr.
You are pretty . . ."

He stopped when he saw my mother coming down the stairs, me behind her.

"Hey there, Wanda."

"Hi, Poppa," I said in a loud whisper, the knot in my stomach finally coming loose. I was so glad he was all right that I ran down the stairs and threw myself at him.

"August," my mother said, "you owe me an explanation."

"Jane Ann, I'm pretty tired."

"So am I, August. So am I."

"I'll tell you tomorrow. Promise."

"Wanda," my mother said, "you'd best get on to bed."

"Night, Wanda, honey," and then, holding up the bear and waving its paw at me, he said, "This here teddy is for you, honey. Got it in a big Fifth Avenue store up in New York City. Just for you."

"Thank you, Poppa," I whispered, taking the bear from his arms.

"Wanda," Momma said, motioning up the stairs, "you get on to bed. We'll sort all this out in the morning."

My father kissed my cheek and the top of my hair. "See you, Wanda. Love you."

I hugged him quickly and when I passed my mother, I reached out and squeezed her hand. Then I climbed the stairs and went down the hall through my parents' room and into mine. I got into bed, the bear beside me, and looked up at the ceiling. The knot started up again. I thought about my father with that expression on his face, the one my mother hated, waving the bear's paw at me, and I wanted to cry. And when they finally came up to bed, even though I put my pillow over my head and put my hands over my ears, I could hear them.

"Jane Ann," I heard my father say, "okay if I get into bed with you?"

"Do as you please."

"Thanks," he said.

"Did you lose everything?"

No answer.

"Everything?" my mother said.

"Jane Ann," he said, "I don't know what got into me. I swear to God, I don't. One minute I was standing in the store, and the next I was at the airport. I swear I don't know what happened."

— Wonder what I'll do for the rest of the summer. I wish Sarah weren't going to be away all summer. She'd love Mercedes, I know she would, her knowing all those famous people —

"Jane Ann? Did you hear me?"

"Go to sleep, August."

"I can't," he said. "Not with you so mad at me. I swear, Jane Ann, I'll make up all those receipts."

"How?"

"I'll find a way."

— I wonder if Mercedes knows movie stars. There are a lot of movie stars up in New York and she's been there —

"Go to sleep, Aug."

"Jane Ann," he said. "I swear to you this night, I'll never take another drink. I swear to you."

"I'm tired of hearing that. Go to sleep."

— *Maybe I'll ask her.*

"But I mean it, Jane Ann. This time I mean it. I've got Wanda to think of. She deserves to be thought of."

"If she deserves to be thought of, then let her sleep."

"Jane Ann," he said, "did you see that big bear I brought her? It's almost as big as she is."

"Oh, Aug, stop it. Please stop it. You use a month's receipts for a trip to New York and bring home something that probably cost half the receipts and expect me to be pleased. Please. Please. Just go to sleep."

— *Maybe she knows Tom Jones.*

"Jane Ann," my father said. "I love you a whole lot. A whole lot."

— *Maybe even Gene Kelly.*

"I'm going down to the parlor," my mother said.

— *I'm going to ask her tomorrow. Tomorrow that's just what I'm going to do.*

Then I put my arms around the bear, turned toward the wall, and went to sleep.

Chapter 5

When Poppa finally came down to the kitchen that next morning, his eyes kept opening up as if somebody were popping flashbulbs two inches from his face.

"Morning, Wanda," he said.

"Morning, Poppa."

"How'd you like the bear?" he whispered, being careful not to let my mother hear. "Always promised you a big one. Right?"

"Right, Poppa," I whispered, looking over at Momma before giving him a quick hug. "I like it fine."

"Morning, Jane Ann," he said in a very low, almost sorrowful voice.

I hated to be with them at times like this. Momma would get all stiff, and whatever she said shot out of her mouth like she was a human cap gun. And Poppa would put on a sad look and do whatever he thought my mother wanted him to do. I didn't like it when he did that. I didn't like to see him like a sad little boy.

"Okay if I bring Mercedes a cup of coffee?" I asked.

"That'd be nice, Wanda," she said, talking to me but looking over at my father. "It's good and strong."

"Does she take sugar?" I asked.

"I believe she takes two sugars. Yes, I believe she does. Bring her a muffin, too. Fresh out of the oven," she said. Again talking to me but looking over at my father. That was her way of telling my father there were muffins for breakfast.

"Thanks, Momma."

"Well, it's the least I can do. She surely has been a great comfort to me these past days."

It pleased me to hear my mother talk like that, even though she was saying it for my father to hear and feel sorry about. Usually she said she didn't need anybody. And whenever she said that, I felt like we were all a bunch of strange people living in a big, old, strange house. It was true in a way, what with April May and the rest of them, but when my mother said things like that, I felt really lonely.

Whenever Sarah invited me over to her house, there wasn't a room we couldn't go into. Except her parents'. We'd fix our nails or we'd try a new hairstyle. Or we'd paint each other's toenails. Her mother never made a big thing about my being there. I was just there. But when Sarah came to my house, it was different. My mother would get all fussed up, trying to look relaxed. She'd keep smoothing her hair or fixing her dress. Then she'd say she'd just waxed the hall floor, and did we mind staying out on the porch? "Or maybe you girls would like to go for a walk. It's such a fine day," she'd say.

Most times, we'd end up going over to Sarah's or we'd walk down to the five-and-dime and look for some new nail polish.

"Momma," I'd say when Sarah left, "Sarah doesn't care what goes on here. She's my friend. My best friend."

But my mother would say, "I know. But it's best not to let anybody see your dirty linen." And the dirty linen Momma was talking about was Poppa. I hated her for thinking about Poppa that way. But sometimes I hated Poppa, too, for what he did. He was always promising never to do it again. He'd promise Momma he was going to go to meetings to help him stop and that one day she'd be free of the boarders and able to finish up her teaching certificate. But she never believed him and Poppa knew it. Mercedes had told me that Poppa was the one who had to believe it. "It'd be a nice thing if your momma did, but don't let that stop you from believing," she'd told me. And I do believe. I think.

I finished fixing Mercedes's tray and started upstairs.

"Wanda," my mother said, "make sure you don't leave crumbs up there. We don't want April May's problem up in the attic."

"Yes, Momma."

April May was standing in her doorway and when

she saw the tray, she said, "Well, ain't that nice of you, Wanda. I was just fixing to go on down and fix myself some breakfast."

"This is for Mercedes. Momma said to bring it on up."

"Momma said to bring it on up," she said. "Well, I declare, ain't that something. I swear to the Almighty, blood means nothing in this house. A perfect stranger, not here a week, and she gets served like she's something special."

"She is," I said, starting up to the attic.

"Well, there are those of us who would heartily dispute that."

I didn't answer her but kept on going upstairs.

"Did you hear me, Miss High and Mighty?"

"I heard you."

"I ain't like your momma, 'cause even if I was down to my last penny, I wouldn't let her or her kind in my home."

"Sticks and stones can break her bones, but names will never hurt her," I called back.

"God Almighty," she said, "you're beginning to sound like Calvin."

"Somebody calling for me?" Mr. Collins called from the bathroom. "I'll be out in just a moment or two."

"No," April May yelled. "Nobody's calling for you." Then she slammed her door. Hard.

I tapped on Mercedes's door with my foot. "Mercedes," I said, "you up yet?"

"Am I up yet?" she said, opening the door. "A body would find it pretty hard to sleep in around here."

Then, looking at the tray, she smiled and took it from me. "Well, isn't this nice. Does your momma know you took this on up?"

I nodded. "She put the muffins and jam out for you."

"Well, this *is* nice," she said, putting the tray on the table beside the rocker. "Come share it with me."

I sat on the floor in front of the rocker and watched her fix her coffee. She did take two spoonfuls of sugar. She put it to her lips, closed her eyes, and drank some. "Wonderful," she said. "Absolutely wonderful."

She buttered the muffins and handed me one. "Here. Better put it on a napkin."

We sat and ate the muffins and Mercedes shared her coffee with me. I hardly ever drank coffee before, but sitting with her and eating muffins and talking, it did taste wonderful.

"Well," she said, wiping her mouth. "That was a treat. Thanks a lot, hon."

She got up, opened her purse, and took out some cigarettes.

"You smoke?" I said.

"Just a few," she said. "Used to smoke two packs a day, but no more. It's bad for you."

She opened the window. "Think your momma will mind?"

I shrugged.

"They say you always remember who gets you started on bad habits," she said. "It's true. I remember his name. Elvus."

"You know him? You know Elvis? *The* Elvis?" I said, jumping up from the floor.

"No, not that Elvis," she said. "It was Elvus, E-L-V-U-S Smith from Monk's Creek, who got me started smoking."

"Oh," I said, sitting back down on the floor, my whole body slumping down almost to my feet. "I thought maybe you knew Elvis himself. You said you knew famous people."

"So who said I didn't know *the* Elvis? Did I say that?"

I jumped up again. "You mean it, Mercedes? Do you know him?"

She nodded her head. "Someday I'll tell you about it. But right now, sweetie, I got to get me dressed. I've got me another rehearsal in Savannah in just about one hour."

"Please," I said, "just answer me one thing. Did you ever talk to him? Not just see him on a stage or something."

She got up, stretched her arms, and said, "Honey, I went to school with old Elvis. To Humes High School." She put up two fingers, winked at me, and said, "For a time, Elvis and me were like this."

"Did you know he's my favorite? Sarah's, too. Our very favorite. Sarah's got all his albums. I've just got one. Poppa promised to get me another one. Wait till she hears this. She'll die. She'll just about die."

"Now, hon, don't you go bragging on this," Mercedes said.

I nodded. "Promise you'll tell me all about it?"

"Sure, honey. Sure I will. I might even have an old picture of me and him," she said.

"Oh, God," I said, "Sarah's really going to die. Me, too."

"Go on, now," she said, brushing crumbs onto the tray before handing it to me. "I've got to get me dressed."

I floated down the stairs, and when I passed April May's door, she was standing there waiting for me.

"Well," she said, "did your fine lady enjoy her breakfast?"

"She sure did. And you'd never guess who she went to school with. You'd never guess in a million years."

"Her kind don't go to school. Besides, I don't like guessing games."

"I'm not asking you to guess 'cause it's just between Mercedes and me."

"Just between Mercedes and me," she mimicked. "She's lying. I declare, your momma is something letting you associate with the likes of her. If you were my child, you know what I'd do?"

I didn't answer her. It was useless. Instead I said to her in a real sweet voice, "Mr. Murphy picking you up today, April May? He taking you out for a drive?"

"What's your interest in Murph?" she asked.

"Just wondering," I said.

"Well, for your information, he is coming on by, and I'll thank you to be as polite to him as you are to that one upstairs. 'Cause one of these days, Murph is going to come into quite a tidy sum of money, and I'll be nothing but a memory here."

"A bad one," I said under my breath. And then I said, "Better not let Mr. Murphy meet Mercedes."

"Why?"

"Because she's so pretty, Mr. Murphy's two front candles might just drop right out of his mouth." And before she could answer, I ran as fast as I could down the stairs and toward the kitchen.

"Pretty is as pretty does, child," Mr. Collins called from his room.

"Will you shut up, Calvin?" she yelled. "Just shut up!" And April May's door slammed so hard, my parents' wedding picture fell off the downstairs wall and smashed onto the hall floor.

Chapter 6

"I surely am tired of these goings-on," my mother said, picking up the pieces of glass that had fallen from her wedding picture. "April May," she called up, "if you slam that door one more time, you are going to find yourself out of this house. Do I make myself clear?"

April May didn't answer.

"April May," my mother called again, "did you hear me?"

My father came in from the kitchen and began to help my mother pick up the pieces, trying so hard to get in her good graces.

"Jane Ann," he said quietly, "I know how hard it is for you having April May here."

"That's not all that's hard."

"Well, I've been thinking there's got to be a way to get Mr. Murphy to pop the question."

She didn't answer him.

"Jane Ann?" he said. "You hearing me?"

"He doesn't have two nickels to his name," she said in her cap gun voice. "They'll end up living here."

"Don't you remember? His momma owns a farm back in Claxton. I heard him tell April May she was going to sign it over to him. And he's crazy about April May. A fact I cannot figure out, but a true fact."

Momma picked up the last of the glass and looked at her wedding picture quickly before putting it on the hall table. "Wanda," she said, "would you take this on down to Mr. Trask so's he can put new glass in it? And make sure he gives you a receipt. April May's going to pay."

"Jane Ann," my father said, "will you listen to me? I'm going to figure out a way to get Henry to make April May Dohr, April May Murphy."

"What would folks say?" my mother said. "April May married to Mr. Murphy. Bad enough what's said when they see them picnicking on the front lawn."

We hardly had any neighbors and Momma never bothered with those we had, but she was always worrying about what they were thinking about us. Like they were going to stop being friends with her.

"I'm telling you, Jane Ann. There's a way and I'm going to find it. Before you know it, April May'll be off for Claxton."

My mother nodded and started upstairs. "Well, first I'm going to give her a piece of my mind."

The door to Mr. Collins's room was open and when he heard my mother's voice, he came to the top of the stairs. He was wearing his old plaid bathrobe and faded maroon felt slippers. His gray hair was sticking up like the top of a candy kiss. "Aah, dear lady," he said to my mother, "strength is a matter of the made-up mind."

When Momma got into April May's room I could hear April May carrying on, accusing my mother of favoring all the other boarders. "It ain't like I don't pay my way," she said. "I pay eleven dollars every other Friday. Like clockwork. And you never hear me complain about the extra seventy-five cents you sneak in. Have you?"

"And what about all the iced drinks?" my mother asked. "And the birdseed? And the cream for your coffee? And fresh towels and linens and soap?"

"Soap?" April May said. "Why, in all my days I never have seen the likes of the soap." And then, imitating my mother's voice, she said, "Wanda, honey, make sure you cut the Ivory bar into three pieces, else they leave it all over and waste it."

"You are most ungrateful," my mother said.

"Well, you won't have old April May to push around much longer," April May said. "Soon as Murph's ship comes in, I am out of here. And then you two will be up Shit Creek . . ."

Even though I couldn't see my mother, I could see her face. Red with her eyes popping out of her head.

"April May," she said, her voice getting louder. "I will not have that kind of talk around here. I have other guests in my home."

"Guests? You call what you rented your own daughter's room to a guest? She's a damn liar. Why, she's nothing but a . . ."

The door to April May's room slammed and I heard Momma's voice rise and fall, but I couldn't hear what she was saying. After a long while, the door opened and Momma said in a loud voice, "And for the time you remain here, April May, I'll thank you to act like a guest. A paying one. But a guest nonetheless."

"April May," Mr. Collins called out, "Shakespeare must have been referring to you when he said, 'Unbidden guests are often welcomest when they are gone.'"

I didn't hear April May's answer, but I thought I heard my mother whisper, "Oh, hush up, Calvin."

Before I could ask Momma why April May talked so poorly about Mercedes, she swept by me and on out into the kitchen. "August," she called, "your sister has gone too far this time —"

I went into the dining room and sat down and waited for Mercedes to come downstairs, and when I heard her coming, I grabbed the wedding picture from the hall table and started out the door. She came out wearing the prettiest summer dress I'd ever seen. It was pale yellow with a big white collar and little white flowers down the front. She had her hair piled up high and she was wearing shiny white high heels. She looked around, took a deep breath, swung her straw bag over her shoulder, and started down the steps.

"Mercedes," I called. "Wait up. I've got to walk downtown, too."

She turned around, smiled, and when I caught up with her, we started to town.

"Mercedes, please, please tell me how you met him."

"I told you, hon. This is a busy morning for me. I've got me a date in Savannah. I've got no time right now."

"But you can talk while we're walking. You can do that, can't you?"

She smiled at me and nodded. "Well, what do you want to know?"

"About Elvis. What was he like?"

"Like? Why, he was just about the prettiest boy I ever saw. Big soft eyes and smooth white skin. But it was his hair that got me."

"His hair?"

"He'd comb that hair all the time. Or fix it with his hands. That's still how I picture him. Fixing his hair."

"Oh, God," I said. "You actually saw him comb his hair."

"Listen, hon," she said, walking a little bit faster. "I've got to get me down to that bus stop or I'll be late for my own rehearsal."

I walked faster to keep up with her, trying to get her to tell me more, but she kept saying she was rushed and that she'd tell me more when she got back. "You just wait, hon. I know more people than just Elvis. You know Little Richard?"

I shook my head.

"I cannot believe you never heard of Little Richard," she said. "Why, he's a big star, too."

I didn't care about anybody else. All I cared about was hearing more about Elvis.

"Mercedes," I said, "you think you'll ever get to see him again?"

She shook her head and ran for the bus.

"Why not?" I yelled, running after her. "You could go to your high school reunion, maybe."

"Oh, sweetie," she said, holding her bag tight and waving for the bus driver to wait for her, "shush now."

When the bus stopped in front of us, I said, "Will you tell me more?"

She nodded her head, picked up her skirt just a bit, and boarded the bus.

"Everything?" I yelled.

"Everything," she called back.

I kicked up some gravel and smiled to myself; then I started down to Mr. Trask's shop. When I got there, he was putting the window awning down. "Mornin', Wanda," he said. "Be with you in just a second."

I put my mother and father's wedding picture down on the counter and looked at it, really looked at it for the first time. I did look like Momma. Poppa always said I did, but I'd never seen it before. I rubbed my hand over the surface and felt something sharp. So sharp it almost cut my finger. I looked closer and saw that the glass had cut a slit right down the center of the picture.

"How you been, Wanda? Ain't seen you in quite a spell."

"Fine," I said, still looking at the picture.

"What have we got here?" he said, taking the picture

from the counter. "Picture seems to be comin' apart. No problem fixin' that. Frame seems fine. How about pickin' it up on Saturday?"

I nodded my head. "My mother wants the receipt, please."

"You tell your momma I always give receipts," he said, turning his back to me.

I thanked him and started home.

— *I hope Momma is really talking to Poppa. Not just the way she was doing this morning. But really talking to him. Maybe he's left and he's at the shop. Maybe I should stop by to see him.*

"Wanda. Wanda," I heard somebody call. I turned and saw Mr. Trask hurrying down the sidewalk, waving something.

"Girl," he said, "what's gotten into you? You asked for a receipt, I write one up, and you walk out on me."

"Sorry," I said, "I was thinking about something else."

"Just what your mother needs," he said. "Another daydreamer."

Chapter 7

"Wanda," my mother called when I came in the front door. "Did you get a receipt from Mr. Trask?"

"Yes," I said. "I'll leave it on the hall table."

She came out of the kitchen, her hair falling down over her eyes, the strings to her apron hanging down. "Whew," she said, "I'll be happy to finish up that dirty old oven. Takes all my strength these days to get it shining again."

I started upstairs but turned back and said, "Momma, what did April May say to you this morning that got you so fussed up?"

"Oh, you know April May," she said. "She's got her own ideas on things."

"Like what?"

"Oh, it's not worth talking about, hon. You go on now. I'm going to finish up in the kitchen." And before I could ask her anything else, she was gone.

I went upstairs and looked out the window in the hall, hoping to see Mercedes walking down the street, but I knew it was way too early.

— I wonder if she could get a gig with Elvis. I never heard her sing but I would bet anything she's good.

April May's door was opened a little and I could hear her talking to Petey, telling him how he belonged to her and only to her. And I could hear Mr. Collins calling to her that no living thing ever truly belongs to another living thing.

"Shut up, Calvin," she said, slamming her door. Then she opened and closed it again, quietly.

When I passed Mr. Collins's room, he was standing in the doorway, still wearing his bathrobe and slippers. "Wanda," he said, "you know that, don't you?" And before I could ask him what he was talking about, he said, "Nobody can own another's soul. Not even a bird's."

I smiled at him and walked down the hall, through my parents' room and into mine. I closed the door behind me and pulled the shade down. Tight.

I stretched out on my bed, and when I looked at Elvis's picture on my dresser, it made me think of Sarah. I wished she were here. I could tell Sarah things I couldn't tell anybody else. I wondered what she was doing now. She told me her father had promised to take her to Hollywood when they got to California. I wondered if Mercedes had ever been there. My father had promised me he'd take me there someday. He promised lots of things that didn't seem ever to happen. Like how I was going to get to sleep in my own room again. "Wanda, honey," he'd said the day he'd put the shade on the glass door in my room, "this is temporary. Only temporary. I swear to you, honey, soon as business picks up you're going to be sleeping like a princess."

Momma told me it wasn't the business that needed picking up, it was Poppa.

"Wanda," I heard my mother call. "Are you okay?"

"Yes. I'm fine."

I could hear her coming on through her bedroom toward mine.

"I'm coming on in," she said.

And before I could say no, there she was.

"Wanda," she said, "I'll be needing for you to take Poppa's lunch on down to the shop. He went out of here without it and he doesn't have as much as twenty-five cents in his pocket. You know what he said to me this morning?"

I shook my head.

" 'Jane Ann,' he said, 'I'm not going to have as much as a quarter in my pocket at any given time. No,' he said, 'I am keeping away from temptation.' "

"That's good, Momma."

"Oh, Lord," she said, shaking her head back and forth slowly. "He means what he says when he says it, but then . . ."

"Maybe this time it'll be different," I said. But I didn't want to talk about it.

"You think so, Wanda?"

"Yes," I said. "I think so."

"Well," she said, "soon as I have his lunch ready you'd better get on down. He'll be waiting. That okay, Wanda?"

I nodded. The taking-the-lunch-down-to-the-shop thing was something else I hated. It was Momma's way of checking up on Poppa after he'd gotten into trouble, only she never was the one to do it. It was always me. Poppa would smile and shrug and say, "Thank you kindly, Wanda. Tell Momma I am here with my nose to the grindstone." Then he'd look over at me and say, "Excuse me. Sinkstone." There were times when he wasn't there. He'd be over at MacPherson's, but I wouldn't tell my mother. I hated that even more, lying to her, but it was better than telling her because when she heard it, it wasn't as though she'd go on down to the shop. She'd wait at home. And when he came in, it would start. It was better not to tell. Sometimes when he got home he wouldn't be so bad, and he could fool even her.

My mother looked over at the bear my father had brought home. "Look at that silly thing," she said. "Look at the size of it."

Then she came over and sat on the bed. She rubbed the bear's head and fingered the bow around his neck. "This is probably one half of the month's receipts. Miz Plum's toilet. Miz Love's sink. And our table money."

"Oh, Momma," I said. "Can't you forget it? Poppa said he was going to try harder."

She shrugged. "I know. It's just that it's happening more often." Then she got up and closed the door and came over and sat next to me and said, "Can you keep a secret?"

"Sure, Momma," I said. "But if it's about April May and Mr. Murphy, I heard Poppa this morning. I was there. Remember?"

"It's not that," she said, putting her arm around my shoulder. "I've got something else I want to tell you. Poppa doesn't even know." My stomach began to knot.

"Wanda," she said, her face as serious as I'd ever seen it. "Wanda, honey, what would you think about having a sister? Or maybe a brother?"

I slid away from her and sank back on my bed, my back leaning against the bear, its paw resting on my arm. I couldn't believe her. I thought she was going to tell me she was going to ask Poppa to live down at the shop for a while, like she'd done when he'd taken the trip to Charlottesville, which wasn't as bad as the trip to New York.

"Well," she said, "what do you think?"

I couldn't understand her at all. Always complaining about how many mouths she had to feed and how much things cost and how shoes were getting to be like golden slippers. And here she was talking about having a baby.

"Momma," I said, "I don't think you ought to be thinking like that."

She kind of slumped down and looked at me with a funny expression on her face. "Well, it's kind of late for that," she said. "I'm on my way. Well on my way."

"Where? What are you talking about, Momma?"

"I'm going to have a baby come October." Tears came to her eyes and her mouth began to quiver.

"Maybe this is just what Poppa needs. More responsibility. Besides, I can't do anything about it, Wanda. What is, is."

I wanted to reach out to her, to tell her everything would be just fine, but I couldn't. I pushed myself back into the bear and wrapped its arms around me.

She got up and started out the door. "I'll have Poppa's lunch ready in ten minutes." And then she was gone.

— This is a crazy place. A crazy place. I used to beg Momma to get me a sister or a brother. "What?" she'd say. "That's the last thing we need around here." And Poppa would say things like "Maybe someday, Wanda. Maybe someday."

I wonder if Mercedes has a sister. Or a brother. I think Elvis was an only child. But I think that was because he was a twin and the other twin died. Mercedes would know about that. Poppa was an only child until April May came along. "And to think I prayed so hard to have a little brother or sister," Poppa would say. "It surely is true you better be darn sure you want what you pray for. Because you just might get it."

"Wanda," my mother called, "Poppa's lunch is ready."

I took my time going down to the shop. All sorts of things were going through my head. Like where the baby was going to sleep and how was Momma going to take care of a baby with all she had to do. I didn't want a baby around. I knew what would happen. I'd end up doing all the work. But it wasn't even that. It was something else. I'd never get out of Harmony. I'd be just like my mother. Probably running a boardinghouse. Pushing myself to do things I really didn't want to do. I'd never even get my room back. I thought about Sarah and how much I missed her and how lucky she was.

I walked by the bus stop, hoping to see Mercedes, but she wasn't there. Then I took the long way to Poppa's shop and when I got there, Poppa was all alone. "George is at Miz Plum's again. That darn toilet is giving her trouble. Seems like it just won't stop running."

I handed Poppa his lunch and when I did something jingled in the bag. He opened it, peeked in, and pulled out a small envelope. He read the front of it and smiled. "Momma sent me a dollar in change," he said. "She says no man should be without money in his pocket."

I smiled back and kind of shook my head. I just couldn't understand her at all. She confused me. Especially with Poppa. One minute telling me one thing and the next minute doing something else. And now her having a baby.

"Momma said supper is going to be at five-thirty."

He started eating his lunch and before I left, he said, "Now you be sure to tell Momma I'm here working my fingers to the bone." Then he kissed me on the cheek, messed up my hair, and said, "You're my girl, Wanda."

"Poppa," I said, wanting to ask him how he felt about the baby, but then I remembered Momma hadn't told him yet. "Don't forget. Supper at five-thirty."

I kissed him good-bye and went out the door and back to the bus stop. I decided I'd wait for Mercedes. Right now, I needed to be by myself. Besides, if I went home my mother would be giving me something to do. Like changing the linen. Or bringing up fresh towels to everybody. Or straightening up the bathroom. Or asking me how Poppa looked. And did I smell anything that I wasn't supposed to smell?

The day was sunny and the air was warm. I sat on the park bench opposite the bus stop, letting the warm sun shine on my face, and closed my eyes. "Daydreaming again, Wanda," my mother always said. "Nights are for dreaming." But my father was different. "That's the nicest part of the day, Wanda. Daydreaming. The time between wake time and real dreams."

— I wonder when Mercedes will show me the picture of Elvis. Maybe she'll give it to me. Or make me a copy. Wouldn't that be something?

Then I thought about April May and how nasty she talked about Mercedes.

— Maybe I should tell Mercedes she's like that to everybody, except Mr. Murphy.

A bus pulled in and I jumped up and ran across to the bus stop, but she wasn't on it. I went back to the bench and waited and when her bus finally came and she got off, she waved to me and called, "Just the one I was hoping would be waiting."

"Why?" I said.

"Why?" she said. "'Cause you being here is nice. And besides, I've got a lot of telling to do. Don't I?"

"You sure do," I said. And then the two of us walked down Decatur Avenue, onto Lotus Lane, and on down to Marigold Place and home.

Chapter 8

"And just where did you hide yourself this afternoon?" my mother asked as we came on up the walk. "I called Poppa and he told me you left the shop at one o'clock. Then I telephoned Sarah. I tried all afternoon and there was no answer."

"They're away," I said.

"You never told me . . ."

"Sorry, Momma," I said.

"Well, where were you?"

"I waited for Mercedes."

"Well, see that you don't do that again without telling me."

"I won't."

"Promise?"

"Promise."

"Thank you," she said. Then she smiled over at Mercedes and said, "My, isn't that a pretty dress. Makes you look like a yellow rose."

Mercedes laughed a little. "I've been called lots of things in my life, but that's the first time I've ever been called a rose."

Mr. Collins was sitting on the glider, and when he heard Mercedes's voice, he called out, "'What's in a name? That which we call a rose By any other name would smell as sweet . . .'"

"'I take thee at thy word: Call me but love, and I'll be new baptized . . .'"

Mr. Collins stood up, put his hand on his chest, and said, "O! swear not by the moon, the inconstant moon, That monthly changes in her circled orb, Lest that thy love prove likewise variable.'"

"'. . . Good night, good night!'" Mercedes said, looking up at Mr. Collins. "As sweet repose and rest Come to thy heart as that within my breast . . .'"

"Oh, dear lady," Mr. Collins said, his face flushed, his eyes sparkling, "you are a student of the Bard."

"Oh, no, not me. Not Mercedes," she said. "That's the only Shakespeare I know. I remember it because it was the only time I ever stayed in one place long enough to be part of anything that happened in school. I was Romeo's stand-in." She laughed out loud. "Excuse me," she said, "I was second stand-in. John Lee Durant was first."

"It matters not, dear lady," he said. "You have filled my day with sunshine and blessed me with a memory." Then he bowed and said, "James Barrie said, 'God gave us memories that we might have roses in December.'

You, dear lady, will be remembered till my last December comes."

"That was lovely, Mr. Collins," my mother said. "Just lovely."

"Just what we need around here," April May called from her window. "More hogwash."

"You be still up there," Momma said. "It'll keep you out of trouble."

"Watcha doin'? Watcha doin'?"

"And you know what Elbert Hubbard said about trouble, April May?" Mr. Collins called out.

But before he could tell her, April May told him to shut up and put her window down. Not hard. But hard enough.

"Well, I'm going to take me upstairs," Mercedes said. "You want to come on up?"

I nodded and followed her.

"Not too long now, Wanda," Momma said. "I'll need the table set for supper."

Momma never gave up. It seemed sometimes she enjoyed spoiling people's fun.

"I know, Momma."

"Sweetie," Mercedes said, when we walked into her room, "do me a favor, will you?"

"Sure," I said.

"Pass me those flat slippers over yonder in the corner. My feet are killing me. My shoes feel like they are going to squeeze my feet to death."

She sank down on the bed, put some cream on her feet and rubbed them. "Aaah," she said, "that feels good. Makes me think of my momma. She stood on her feet all day. Every day. Seems to me her feet were always hurting her."

"What'd she do?"

"What'd she do? She had eight babies. That's what she did."

"Eight?"

"Eight that lived. Seems to me she had one that died before it was born."

"That's funny," I said.

"What's funny about that?"

"Not that," I said. "But just today I got to wondering if you had any brothers or sisters."

"Three brothers. Four sisters. And I'm the oldest," Mercedes said. "Terrible to be the oldest in a big family. Swore I'd never have any children after I got out of that house."

"You probably would have made a good momma," I said.

She shrugged and said, "Maybe. But I'm not a momma. And so that's that."

She went over to the window and opened it wide and sat in the rocker. "Something bothering you?" she said. "You look like you're carrying something heavy."

I shook my head. And then blurted out, "Momma's going to have a baby."

"Those things do happen, hon. Especially to married folk."

"But it's different with Momma and Poppa," I said. "Momma's always saying that things are bad and that Poppa doesn't make enough money and that she's tired of taking in boarders . . ."

"Well," she said, "it seems to me somebody like your momma kind of knows what she's doing."

"She didn't even tell Poppa," I said.

"She will. In her own time." Mercedes settled herself back in the rocker and said, "But there's something more bothering you than that."

I pretended I didn't hear her. I didn't even know exactly what was bothering me. Maybe it was Poppa. Or maybe it was hearing Momma and April May fighting over Mercedes and then Momma closing the door and all. It wasn't like Momma to fight like that.

"Anytime you want to talk, hon, you remember I'm here."

"I'll remember," I said. "But remember what you said? You said you'd tell me everything about Elvis. Everything."

She rocked a little and leaned back in the chair. "Well," she said, starting out very slowly, "I was about fifteen when I met him. Little bit older than you. We'd just moved from Monk's Creek to Memphis. My father — my stepfather, I mean — was a drifter. Drank, too. He was okay when he didn't drink, but when he did, we had to watch out. We'd go from town to town, him looking for work."

"What happened to your real poppa?"

"Oh, sweetie, that's another story," she said, with a

faraway look in her eyes. "Funny, I thought I'd never do that. Drift around. I swore I'd settle down in one place and make friends I'd have forever."

"At least you get to see all sorts of places."

"I guess," she said, "but maybe there are other ways. Like staying on someplace. Not roaming."

"Maybe you will someday."

She nodded slowly, then said, "Now what do you want to know about Elvis?"

"What was the actual day you met him?"

"I guess it was the day I registered at the high school. I was scared. Ever feel that way, Wanda?"

"Sometimes," I said. "Most of the time."

"But I wanted to go to that school so bad —"

"How come? Did you know Elvis went there?"

"No. How would I know that? I just wanted to go to a school where I could really learn something."

"You can do that anywhere."

She looked at me and shook her head. "Well, anyway, I went all by myself, scared and all. Momma had to bring the rest of the kids to grade school, so I even registered myself. They put me in as a junior. Tested me first. Would you believe I was the youngest one in that class? Kind of pushed me ahead. Surprised me. I never thought I had any kind of brains before that."

I pushed closer to the rocker.

"Anyway, I went down to Miss Fitzhugh's class and there he was. Sitting in the back row. Prettiest boy I ever saw."

"What'd he do when he saw you?"

"Nothing. What'd you expect him to do? Him sitting in class."

"Did he look at you?"

"I don't remember. But I do remember one thing. His hair. I told you that, didn't I?"

I nodded.

"But it was the nicest head of hair I'd ever seen. He kept patting it down. Seemed like his hands never left his hair. And I do remember his smile. What a smile."

"More," I said, inching closer. "More."

"Miss Fitzhugh, the teacher they put me in the class with, one of those long-nosed, skinny ladies who always looked as though they were having pain somewhere, introduced me to the class. I can remember her words as if it were yesterday." Then Mercedes looked beyond me and out through the window and said softly, " 'This is our new student, Mercedes McIver.' "

"Why'd she call you that instead of Mercedes Washington?"

But Mercedes didn't answer me. She rocked for a long while, looking through the window as though she were back in that school. I just sat waiting. Then she nodded and said, "Yes, she was the first person who said Mercedes like I say it now. I never forgot that."

"What did Elvis do?"

"Oh, sweetie, I don't remember. Maybe he smiled at me. Maybe he didn't. There were other kids in that room."

"What did you do?"

"I sat there wondering how long I'd be in that school. I knew I wouldn't be there long. And sure enough, in about two months I was out. Wasn't anything I wasn't used to, but oh, God, I sure hated to leave that place. Like I said to Mr. Collins, that was the first place I felt part of anything." She leaned back and closed her eyes and let out a big sigh. "That's where I got my picture taken with Elvis."

"Oh, God," I said. "You mean it? You and Elvis? Sarah will not believe this."

"Sweetie," Mercedes said, "there are forty-two people in that picture and I am just about hidden behind forty of them."

"I don't care," I said. "I would die to be on the same stage with him. The only one I've ever been onstage with is Gerard Flitty. And who even knows him? But how many people can say they actually were on the same stage with Elvis?"

"At least forty-two," she said.

"Did Elvis miss you when you left?"

"I was only there two months."

"Did he give you something to remember him by?"

Mercedes laughed out loud. "Wanda, if you aren't the biggest dreamer in the entire state of Georgia, I'm a groundhog waiting to see my shadow."

"Where is it?"

"Where is what?"

"The picture!"

"It's in one of my bags. Just as soon as I come across it, I'll show it to you. But for now, sweet bun, I have got to get me some rest. I've got two shows to do tonight. And it's a long way by bus."

"Mr. Gingrich has a car," I said. "Maybe he'll take you."

"I couldn't ask him to do that," she said. "I'm planning on renting a car soon as I get my first check."

"I can ask him," I said.

"You think he'd mind?"

I shook my head. "No," I said. "Before Mr. Gingrich got a car, Poppa took him places."

"Maybe I could ask your poppa. I'd pay him."

"Poppa would be glad to take you," I said. "For nothing. But he kind of wrecked the car last winter and Momma wouldn't let him have it fixed. Says it's better that way. But I don't happen to agree with her."

"Wanda, honey," Mercedes said, smiling down at me. "You sound about a hundred and thirteen instead of thirteen. Don't you know that fourteen comes after thirteen, and fifteen comes after fourteen? I thought I sidestepped some of those years along the way, but, lady, you are skipping right through them."

"I'll be fourteen come November," I said.

She shook her head and got up from the rocker and walked over to the closet, taking out one of her stage dresses. "I've got to iron this up for tonight," she said. "Got to sparkle."

"Did you see him after you left?" I said.

"See who?"

"Elvis."

She shook her head.

"Did he write to you?"

She shook her head again and smoothed the beads on the dress she was holding and put it on her bed.

"Did you write to him?"

"Can't remember. Maybe."

"Did he answer you? I'll bet he did."

"Enough. Enough," she said. "I told you I've got me a gig at seven o'clock and here it is a quarter till five and I'm still telling you fairy stories. Out. Out." She led me to the door.

"But Mercedes . . ."

"No *but*'s," she said, "I've got to get me ready."

"Answer me one thing. Just one thing. Did he answer you?"

"Out."

"Did he? Please tell me he wrote to you."

"Okay," she said, "okay. He wrote to me. Now out. O-U-T out."

But before I got down from the attic stairs, she called, "Wanda, you really think Mr. Gingrich would drive me?"

I nodded my head.

"Okay," she said. "But remember what I told you. You don't get nothing for nothing in this life, so tell him Mercedes intends to pay."

Chapter 9

Mr. Gingrich stood in his doorway, nodding. "Sure thing, Wanda," he said. "Why, I'd be happy to do Miz Washington the favor. And you tell her she don't have to pay me, except what it cost me in gas. That's fair. Probably take four, maybe five gallons each way. I'll keep close track of that. Savannah's about forty minutes away, depending on the time of day. We leave here at five-thirty, get there 'long about six-ten, six-fifteen, that is, if there's no traffic. Today's Friday. Probably heavier today than usual. Then there's the trip back. If it's real late, it'll take less time. That's a plus, but I'm a person who don't like to travel on the highways much after eleven. Hhmmmnnn. What time she say she's going to be finished with work?"

"She didn't."

"Well," he said, "don't do much good to stand here worrying about that. Person needs a favor, I'm glad to do it. Guess I can take in a show and get me some supper. Haven't been to Savannah in five years or so.

Maybe do me some good," he said, rummaging around in his pockets for his pipe. "You want to come along, Wanda? Keep me company in the big city?"

I couldn't believe what he was saying. Me go to Savannah? I'd never been there. Maybe I'd get to hear Mercedes sing.

"You mean that?" I said.

"If it's okay with your momma, it's okay with me."

I raced down the stairs and into the kitchen. Momma was talking in her cap gun voice again. "Is this the thanks I get for feeling sorry that you didn't have some pocket change? 'I'm staying away from temptation, Jane Ann.' That's what you said. 'I'm going to try harder, Jane Ann.' And look at you. Will you look at you?"

Poppa was sitting at the kitchen table, his elbows on the table, his hands across his forehead. "Just had a couple, Jane Ann," he said, quietly.

But even I knew it was more than a couple. His shirt was all wrinkled and he kept shaking his head back and forth, his eyes down, not wanting to look directly at Momma.

"Folks don't get this way on a couple. Where'd you get the rest of the money?"

He didn't answer her, and when he saw me, he said, "Hi, Wanda, honey. How are you?"

"I'm fine, Poppa," I said, but my stomach started jumping around.

"Don't change the subject," my mother said. "Where'd you get the money?"

"From a friend."

"Friend? What kind of friend?"

He shrugged. "Just a friend."

"Well, if it was George Gingrich, he's no friend. And if it was George Gingrich, I'll be asking him to pack up his bags come morning."

I held my breath.

"Jane Ann," he said, "it wasn't George."

I started to breathe again, wanting so much to go to Savannah, wanting so much not to hear Momma and Poppa arguing again.

"You sure? You sure it wasn't George Gingrich? I have ways of finding out."

My father got up and started out the door, my mother after him.

I followed them with my eyes.

"August. August. You come back here."

"Jane Ann," he said, "I've got to get me some sleep."

"But I want to talk with you. Now."

The door to April May's room opened. "Glory be to the Almighty," she said, "can't you let a body be? All he wants to do is get some rest."

"This is none of your business, April May," my mother said.

The door to her room slammed hard, like a gun had been fired. My mother got so rigid it looked like it was she who had been shot. "That's it, April May," she said. "Between this morning and this, you can consider this your month's notice. Do you hear me?"

April May didn't answer her.

"August. August. Are you hearing all of this? I've just given your sister her notice. Do you hear me? Answer me, August."

But he didn't. He just made his way down the hall and into their bedroom.

My mother came back into the kitchen, the door swinging closed behind her. She looked as though she were going to cry. "I mean what I say, Wanda," she said. "Bad enough I've got to put up with your father, but I do not have to put up with April May." Then she wiped her eyes with her apron and said, "One of these days that man is going to go too far and end up in an early grave."

It scared me when she talked like that. I didn't want to hear it again. "Momma," I said quickly, "can I talk to you?"

"Don't you start telling me I'm too hard on Poppa. I don't want to hear it. I'm the one having to deal with him. All of it."

"I know, Momma," I said quietly, wanting so much to escape for a while, knowing when she went upstairs, the arguing would start again. "I know."

She sat at the table and started to rub her hand round and round over the tablecloth. "What'd you want to talk about?"

"Promise you'll listen till I'm finished?"

"I promise."

"Mr. Gingrich's going to drive Mercedes to Savannah in a little while. She's got to be there by seven o'clock."

"What's he doing that for?"

"She can't rent a car until she gets her check and she needs a ride —"

"Oh," she said. "That's kind of him."

"— and he asked me if I wanted to go with them —"

"What?"

"You promised you'd let me finish."

"But Savannah? At this hour?"

"Please, Momma. Please. Maybe I'll get to hear Mercedes sing. You could come, too. I'll bet Mr. Gingrich wouldn't mind. I can ask him."

"We don't know a thing about the kind of club she's singing at."

"Momma, she said it's a fine place."

"What else could she say?"

"She said all sorts of fancy people go there. Even the mayor came the last time she sang there."

She shook her head. "I don't know about this."

"Momma, please. Please, Momma."

She smoothed the tablecloth, flattening out the tiniest wrinkles. "Serve him right if I *did* go," she said in a soft voice. And then she said, "This is the silliest thing I've ever heard. You and me driving into Savannah with Mr. Gingrich. Why, folks just don't take off on a whim."

"Poppa does," I said, using everything I could to get her to say yes. Even Poppa. And then feeling guilty that I'd done it.

She smoothed the tablecloth one more time; then she got up and walked to the cabinet next to the stove.

She reached in and pulled out a covered pot. She took some money out and began counting and when she'd counted the last dollar, she said, "You're right."

Then she came over to where I was sitting and said in a low voice, "You go on up now and ask Mr. Gingrich if he'd mind having me tag along. And don't tell Poppa. You leave the telling to me."

I raced back upstairs to Mr. Gingrich's room. When he told me he'd be pleased to have Momma come along, I ran on up to Mercedes's room. I knocked on the door, hard, and when she said to come in, I burst through the door. "Guess what? We're all going into Savannah. Mr. Gingrich asked me. Momma, too."

"What?" she said, her eyes opening wide. She looked at me for a long minute. Then she smiled and said, "Why, that's nice. It'll be fun having all of you sitting out there. I'm getting to feel closer to you folks than I ever did to mine." Then she turned around and asked me to finish buttoning her dress. It was silver. It had all kinds of beads and sequins sewn on the front and back, and the sleeves were silver clouds. She looked beautiful.

"I don't think we'll be coming to hear you," I said. "We'll probably just have a snack somewhere, then walk around town to see the sights and wait till you're finished. Momma won't spend money on a big supper."

She turned around and put her hands on her hips. "And who said she was going to spend all that money, sweetie? Did I say that?"

She walked over to the mirror and pulled her hair

up, put a silver barrette in it to hold it in place, and then let it fall to her shoulders in a thick ponytail. "How's that?" she said, smiling at herself in the mirror.

"You look beautiful," I said. "You're sparkling."

She turned to me and said, "You got it. And do you know what?"

I shook my head.

"You are all going to be my guests. My honored guests. Why, sweet bun, I'm the headliner of this show."

I could hardly believe my ears. I'd never been out to supper, unless you could call a hamburger at Budd's Diner out to supper. And except for the shows at school and the ones the Ladies' Guild at church put on, I'd never seen a live show before. I laughed out loud. "You mean it, Mercedes? You really mean it?"

"I surely do," she said. "Now you go on down and tell your momma she should dress up a bit. Your poppa and Mr. Gingrich, too."

The laugh left my throat. "Poppa's not going," I said.

"Why not?"

"He's not feeling well."

"Drunk?"

I looked away.

"Well, sweetie, you feeling unhappy about it isn't going to make him any less drunk. Especially when you're going out on the town. Come on, now. You dress up real nice." She walked me to the door. "I've got to finish up my sparkling and you've got to start yours."

I started down the stairs, but before I got halfway

down, she called for me to come on back. When I came into her room she was rummaging through her top dresser drawer. "Aaah," she said, "here it is." Then she turned and put something in the palm of my hand and closed my fingers around it. "I've had this for a long time," she said. "You wear it tonight."

I opened my hand and looked. It was a ring. It was the prettiest ring I'd ever seen. It was silver and shaped like a rose. "But I can't wear —"

"But I want you to. It'll give me good luck," she said. "Besides, it's too small for me. Now out. Out. Out. Out."

I ran down the stairs and down to my bedroom. I opened the door to my parents' room quietly. Poppa was stretched out on the bed, sleeping. That heavy Poppa smell filled the room. His shoes were tucked under the bed and his shirt was off. His pants were on the chair by the bed and he was covered with the summer spread. My mother was standing by her closet. "Shhhh," she whispered. "I just got him settled."

"Mr. Gingrich said he'd be pleased to have you, and Mercedes said to dress up. She's treating us to supper."

Her eyes opened wide and she smiled. She poked her head into her closet and took out the dress she wore whenever she went to church. "This okay?" she whispered.

I nodded.

"What did Poppa say when you told him where we're going?"

She put her finger to her lips. "Shhhh. Don't wake

him." Then she motioned for me to go on into my room. "Wear your pink dress. It's all ironed. Your slip, too," she whispered. "And make sure to wear your good shoes."

I nodded and went into my room. I leaned against the door, shutting it tight, then I opened my hand and looked at the ring again. I slipped it on my finger and held out my hand and smiled. Then I put on my slip and my dress and combed my hair, all the while looking at my finger. I got my good shoes from the closet and put them on. They were tight and when I stood up, they hurt my feet. But I didn't care. I looked in the mirror and held my hand up to my cheek. The ring sparkled and shone. It was more than pretty. It was beautiful. It was the most beautiful thing I'd ever seen. And it made me feel that way, too. Beautiful. Inside and out.

My door opened a crack and my mother whispered, "Wanda. Time to go."

Mr. Gingrich's car was waiting at the foot of the front walk. And even though it was old and the paint was chipping and the back fender was banged in, I felt like Cinderella when he opened the door and helped my mother and me into the backseat.

Mercedes slid into the passenger seat, the skirt of her dress trailing behind. She scooped it in, its silky folds resting on her lap, the beads and sequins shining like a million Milky Ways on a moonless night. "Well," she said, after she'd settled herself, "aren't we the ones." Then she turned and said to my mother, "Miz Dohr, you are a picture."

My mother beamed. "Call me Jane Ann. Please. And I thank you, Mercedes. I thank you kindly."

"You are welcome, Jane Ann. And you, Wanda. Why, you're just the prettiest thing that ever was."

I smiled and thanked her.

Mr. Gingrich started the motor up and we made our way up Marigold Place, onto Lotus Lane, and on up to the highway. Mr. Gingrich was wearing his straw hat and a black suit.

"Mr. Gingrich," Mercedes said, "if I didn't know you, I'd think you were some kind of movie star."

He turned to her, smiled a queer smile, and thanked her. And for the first time since he moved to our house, he didn't say a word. He just smiled that queer smile. After a long time, he got his voice back.

"That building over there is the granary," he said. "Keeps grain fresh as the day it was picked. And that one over there, that big red-brick building, why, that's the main headquarters for the phone company. Hear tell, they got about six hundred people working for them." He laughed and said, "Why, there aren't six hundred people in all of Harmony."

Mercedes laughed. We did, too. It wasn't funny but I guess we were all feeling so good about being in Mr. Gingrich's car, traveling down Route 20 on our way to Savannah, that we felt obliged to laugh. "Yes, sir," he repeated. "There aren't six hundred people in all of Harmony." And we laughed again. And we sang. We laughed and sang all the way to Savannah.

And when we pulled up in front of Le Jazz, Mercedes said, "You be back here about quarter to seven 'cause that's when the first show starts. You'll have to wait till after the show for supper. But I can tell you it's worth the wait."

She slipped out of the car, smoothed her dress, then waved and threw kisses as she disappeared behind a swinging door that said Mercedes Washington — Georgia's Own Sweet Lady of Jazz — Appearing Nightly (Except Sunday) 7 and 9 P.M. — Limited Engagement.

Chapter 10

I sat with my elbows on my knees, my head forward, listening to the master of ceremonies introduce Mercedes.

"And now, ladies and gentlemen, it is my pleasure and privilege to introduce Georgia's own — Miss Mercedes Washington." He started to clap and looked toward the side of the stage. "Georgia sure missed her while she was strutting her stuff up in old Chicago." Then he tucked the microphone under his arm and held out his hand. "Georgia wasn't Georgia without you, Mercedes."

Mercedes swept out from behind the curtain.

"Here she is, ladies and gentlemen, the star of our show — Miss Mercedes Washington." He started to clap again and motioned for the audience to stand up. "Come on, folks, let's give her a real Georgia welcome."

Most everybody stood up. I jumped from my seat and started to clap. So did Momma. Mr. Gingrich, that queer smile on his face, got up and clapped, too.

Momma nudged me and said, "I have never seen anything like this in all my life. Kind of nice knowing she's living right up in our attic."

I could hardly believe my ears. Momma never said anything like that about anybody. Especially not about a boarder.

Momma smiled and looked toward the stage. Mercedes was next to the piano, a big smile on her face, her body still. She stood for a while; then she took the microphone from the master of ceremonies, bowed to him and to the audience. "Thank you, Mr. Jones, and good evening, ladies and gentlemen. It is *so* good to be here. But I want to set the record straight, Mr. Jones. I never left Georgia. Why, I could never do that," she said, putting her hand over her heart. "Because Georgia's right here. Deep inside me. Down to the very littlest bone in my body."

She looked around at the audience, nodding and smiling. Then she motioned to the piano player. The lights dimmed. The music started.

She swayed her shoulders and snapped her fingers, put the microphone close to her face and started to sing. She sounded so good. Better than anybody. Even Miss New, the choir teacher at school. She walked off the stage and down through the audience, smiling at everybody she passed. She hugged the microphone to her like a bouquet of flowers, then she threw her arms out, scattering the bouquet, letting the cord dangle to the floor, and kept singing.

"'— *Have I told you lately that I love you?*' I really do love you folks —"

When she passed our table, she winked at me. Mr. Gingrich got that queer smile again.

"'— *Have I told you lately that I cared?*' I surely do care —"

The room was foggy with smoke and Mercedes's voice drifted over and under the fog, until it was all around us, clear and sweet.

"Can you folks guess what my very favorite song is?" she called out after she'd sung a few songs.

People began to shout at her, and a little man with a cane jumped up, banged his cane on the table and said, "It Had to Be You." Mercedes shook her head.

Then a lady with starched red hair yelled, "Sing 'Melancholy Baby,' Mercedes."

Mercedes shook her head again, walked back to the stage and sat on the piano.

"I think it's terrible the way they're yelling at her," I said.

"She asked them," my mother said. "And it's not bothering her none."

"Well, I think it's rude," I said. Every once in a while, I'd turn around and say "Sshhh," but nobody paid any attention.

Mercedes motioned to the piano player.

"Did I hear anybody ask for this one?" she said.

The lights dimmed again and when the spotlight was right on her she began.

"'*Georgia,*'" she sang, closing her eyes and holding the microphone close to her lips.

"Oooohhh, Georgia,
The whole day through,
Just an old sweet song
Keeps Georgia on my mind —"

The audience started to clap. She kept singing.

"I saiiid, Georgia,
Oooohhh, Georgia,
The soooong of you
Comes as sweet and clear as moonlight
through the pines —
Yeah, yeah, yeah, yeah —"

People in the audience called out to her. She smiled and kept on singing.

"— Other arms reach out to me.
Other eyes smile tenderly —
Still in peaceful dreams I see
That road leads back to youuuuu —"

Some people started to sing along with her. She sang louder.

"— I said, Georgia,
Oooohhh, Georgia,
No peace I find —
Just an old sweet song
Keeps Georgia on my mind."

She slid off the piano and went to the center of the stage and swayed back and forth.

"Other arms, they reach out to me.
Other eyes smile so tenderly . . ."

"Way to go, Mercedes," somebody called out. She nodded and smiled and kept singing.

"— Still in peaceful dreams I see
That road, that road that leads back to you."

She swooped down, came back up again, and slapped her leg, keeping time.

". . . Whooa, Georgia,
Oh, yes, Georgia,
No peace, no peace can I find,
Just an old sweet song
Keeps Georgia on my mind.
Just an old sweet song
Keeps Georgia on my mind . . .
Yeah. Yeah. Yeah. Yeah. Oh yeah."

The audience stood up, clapped, and yelled, "More. More. More."

But Mercedes shook her head, bowed over and over, then thanked them and said, "I've got me a date that I mean to keep."

She walked back to the piano, put the microphone down, and kissed the piano player. I never saw anybody kiss a colored person before. She even gave him a squeeze. Then the master of ceremonies came out with a big bouquet of roses and said, "Thank you, Miss Washington. Thank you."

She kissed him and walked across the stage, down the stairs, and over to our table.

"How'd you like that?" she said, putting the flowers in the center of the table.

"It was just wonderful," my mother said. "Simply wonderful. I don't know when I've enjoyed myself more."

"You were great, Mercedes," I said. "Just great."

"I was, wasn't I," she said. "Good crowd tonight."

She turned to Mr. Gingrich and said, "How about you? You enjoy yourself?"

Mr. Gingrich just nodded and put on that queer smile again.

The waiter brought the menus and I waited for Mercedes to sit down, but she didn't. "You folks will have to excuse me. I've got a date with the piano player. Seems he doesn't know what the key of C is." Then, turning to the waiter, she said, "You make sure you treat my friends in a real proper way."

"We'll wait till you come back to order," I said.

"No, sweetie, I got a feeling this is going to take a while."

"We don't mind waiting, do we, Momma?"

Momma took my hand and said, "Mercedes knows what she has to do." Then she looked up at Mercedes and said softly, "Don't you, Mercedes?"

Mercedes nodded and said, "Now you be sure to order dessert. They are something special."

And even though she smiled at us and her dress sparkled and her hair shone, her eyes looked sad. "Promise?"

"I promise," I said. "I'll save you some."

Then she turned and walked quickly toward the

stage and disappeared behind the curtain, taking some of my good feelings with her.

The menu was so big it took me a long time to figure out what I wanted. Momma ordered stuffed fish and Mr. Gingrich got a steak. I wanted to get something I never had before, so I ordered chicken stuffed with ham and cheese. When it came I could barely eat it because I'd had salad and bread and soup. But when we were finished, just like Mercedes had told us, we ordered dessert. The waiter pushed the dessert cart over to our table. In my whole life, I'd never seen anything like it, trays filled with pies and cakes and chocolate-covered strawberries as big as plums.

After we ordered dessert, Mercedes came back and stood behind Momma, asking us how we enjoyed our supper. "Did they take good care of you?"

"Sure did," Mr. Gingrich said. "How about you? You eat?"

She nodded her head. "I had a bite in the manager's office."

People kept passing by our table, smiling at Mercedes, telling her how much they had enjoyed hearing her sing. I felt like a celebrity. So did Momma. I could tell from the look she had on her face. A little man dressed in a tuxedo came over to her and asked her to sing the "Tennessee Waltz" next time around. "That'll be at the nine o'clock show," she said. Then she said she had to get backstage again, to change for the next show.

"Thanks for the ride, George. No need to wait, though. My friend said he'd lend me his car till I can rent my own. See you all at home. Careful driving, now." She blew kisses and was gone.

The waiter brought our dessert — the strawberries. They dripped with chocolate and when I bit into one the juice spilled into my mouth. Momma said they were heavenly and Mr. Gingrich, his mouth too full to speak, nodded.

When the last strawberry disappeared, Momma leaned over toward me. "Wanda," she whispered, "better call Poppa."

"Poppa?" I said. "Why?"

"To tell him we'll be home in a while."

"But he knows where we are," I said.

She shook her head.

"But you said you'd tell him."

"Well, I didn't," she said, smoothing the tablecloth.

"Why?"

"Why?" she said. "Does Poppa tell me when he gets it into his head to fly on up to New York? Does he?"

"But Momma," I said, "he only does that when he's . . ."

"Well, maybe this will teach him a lesson. Here," she said, putting change in my hand, "go on, now."

"Momma," I said, raising my voice. "Why don't you call him?"

"Shhhh," she said, looking around to see if anybody was listening. "No reason. But I'd just like to sit here and take this all in. I never did have a finer evening."

I knew it was useless. I took the change and started out toward the lobby.

— I wish I weren't in this family sometimes. Sometimes I just plain wish I were somewhere else.

I put the change in the slot and dialed home.

The phone rang for a long time and then somebody picked up the receiver, but nobody said hello. All I could hear were muffled sounds coming from the other end.

"Poppa?" I said. "Poppa, is that you?"

"Wanda?" he said. "Where are you?"

"In Savannah."

"Savannah? Where's Momma?"

"She's here."

"What are you doing in Savannah?" he said, his voice shaking. "Never mind. Doesn't matter. Thank God, you're safe. It's been terrible. Waking up from a sleep, her gone. You with her. Why didn't she tell me? I wouldn't have stopped her."

"I think she forgot."

"Forgot?" he said. He sounded as though he were going to cry.

"Poppa, don't."

"I'm sorry. I'm real sorry. But you've got no idea what I was thinking. She's never done anything like this."

"We'll be home about eleven, Poppa," I said. "We heard Mercedes sing."

He didn't answer me.

"Poppa?"

"I'm here. I'm just so thankful that you and Momma are all right. You've got no idea how scared I was. And April May didn't help any. Said she had no idea where you people were."

"She's lying, Poppa. I saw her sitting in the window when we got into Mr. Gingrich's car."

"George is there with you?"

"Yes, Poppa."

"Oh, God," he said, his voice breaking. "I feel so bad. So bad."

I felt so sorry for him, but I took a deep breath and said, "Poppa. That's the way Momma feels when you —"

"That's past. I swear that's past."

I didn't say anything.

"Wanda, honey, I mean it. I swear to God Almighty I mean it. You'll see. You'll see."

"Yes, Poppa."

"This time, I mean it. I swear I mean it. I've had my last drink."

I wanted to tell him about all the other times he'd said he'd stop. But I didn't. "I'll see you in a while, Poppa."

"I'll be waiting up for you," he said. "You give Momma a kiss for me."

I walked back to the table slowly, thinking about Poppa. Thinking about what he'd said. Thinking about the baby coming and Poppa drinking even then. And then thinking maybe Poppa meant it this time. Maybe.

"What'd he say?" my mother said. "Things okay?"

"He's fine, Momma," I said, picking up Mercedes's roses and putting them to my face. "Just fine."

I took a deep breath, filling myself with the roses; then I leaned over and kissed Momma on the cheek. "That's from Poppa," I said.

"He said to do that?"

I nodded.

She blushed a little. Then she smiled and reached over, squeezed my hand, and said, "Why, thank you, Wanda. Thank you very much."

Chapter 11

"Well," my mother said, settling herself into the backseat of Mr. Gingrich's car, "wasn't that something?"

"It surely was," Mr. Gingrich said, closing the car door. "She sings like a mockingbird on a sweet summer morning."

"She was wonderful," my mother said. "Wasn't she, Wanda?"

I nodded.

She was. The whole night had been wonderful. It was like being at a movie, only I got to eat the food and smell the perfume and touch the flowers.

When Mr. Gingrich started the car, Mercedes ran out of the stage door and over to the car. "Just wanted to tell you again how good it was having you here," she said, smiling at us. "I won't be home for a day or two. They just told me we've got some heavy rehearsing to do." Then she leaned over to Mr. Gingrich and patted his shoulder. "Thanks, George. It was real nice having a ride in."

Mr. Gingrich said it had been his pleasure. I called out "Good night" and my mother kept thanking her over and over for showing us such a wonderful time.

Mercedes waved good-bye one last time and walked back into the club. Mr. Gingrich pulled away from the curb and we headed for home.

I watched the lights of Savannah fade as we sped out of the city. My mother kept saying what a good time she'd had and how good Mercedes sang. Mr. Gingrich kept agreeing with her and after a while, my mother stopped talking, put her head back, and went to sleep. Mr. Gingrich put the car radio on very softly. I was too excited to sleep.

I thought about my father and how he'd said he'd taken his last drink. Wouldn't that be something? Poppa always being the way he was when he didn't drink. Momma happy.

"How about a piece of candy, Wanda?" Mr. Gingrich whispered while he waited for a light to change. "I've got some Life Savers."

I leaned over the front seat and took one from the package. As I did, I saw a big sign, bigger than any sign I'd ever seen. It had a picture of Elvis standing with a microphone in his hand, not holding it the way Mercedes had but holding it out, pointing it at me. Under the picture it said "ELVIS PRESLEY — LIVE IN CONCERT. DEXTER AUDITORIUM. SEPTEMBER 5, 1964. CALL 914-555-1000 FOR YOUR TICKETS. ACT FAST. DON'T WAIT."

"Do you see that?" I whispered to Mr. Gingrich.

"See what?"

"That sign," I said, my voice rising.

"What sign?"

"That sign straight ahead of you," I said. "The one that says Elvis is coming to town."

"Yes, I do, Wanda," he said softly as he pulled away from the light. "Can't say I'm interested one way or another."

"Well, I am," I said real loud.

"Shhh," he said. "Don't want to wake your momma."

I slumped back into my seat. "Please, God," I said to myself, "don't let me forget the number." And then I repeated to myself, over and over, "914-555-1000."

I could hardly wait to tell Mercedes when she got home. And then I remembered she wouldn't be home tonight.

— *Maybe Momma will let me call her at the club. Imagine Elvis coming to the very town where Mercedes is singing. He'll probably come to see her, too. Won't that be something.*

I closed my eyes and whispered, "914-555-1000." Then I imagined Elvis on the stage. I could almost hear him.

— *Mercedes and I are sitting in the front row. She's waving to him, he's waving back. "See you backstage," she says in a loud whisper. He nods. And then the show is over and we go backstage.*

"Elvis," she says when we get to his dressing room, "this

is my friend, Wanda. Wanda Sue Dohr. She's been wanting to meet you."

He looks at me and says, "And I've been wanting to meet you, too. Mercedes here has told me a lot about you." I smile and tell him how much I enjoyed the show. Then he asks Mercedes and me to join him for supper. We say yes and he escorts us to his limousine. He tells his chauffeur to go to the finest restaurant in town.

"Elvis," I say during supper, "I've got this big picture of you on my dresser."

He smiles. His teeth are big and white and beautiful. All of him is beautiful.

"I'm going to paper my room with your posters."

He smiles again. "That means a lot to me," he says, smoothing his hair back again and again, "and I thank you."

"Come on, Wanda," I heard my mother say. "We're almost home."

"We are home," I heard Mr. Gingrich say. "And there's August waiting on the porch for you, Miz Dohr."

I tried to open my eyes, but I couldn't. "914-555-1000," I said. "914-555-1000." Then I heard my father say, "Wanda, honey, come on, now. You've had a long night."

I opened my eyes and said, "914-555-1000. 914-555-1000."

"She must be dreaming, Jane Ann. Dreaming with her eyes open."

Then he led me from the car and into the house. "Need some help going on upstairs?" he said.

I shook my head.

"Good night," he said, kissing my cheek, that heavy smell still with him. "You have a good sleep, now, honey."

"See you in the morning," my mother called.

"914-555-1000," I said as I climbed up the stairs, "914-555-1000."

When I got to my room, I looked for a pencil. I couldn't find one, so I spit on my finger and wrote "914-555-1000" on my window. After I slid out of my dress, I took Elvis's picture off the dresser and put it under my pillow. Then I climbed into bed and fell asleep.

Chapter 12

Momma wouldn't let me call Mercedes at her club. "You can't do things like that," she said. "She's a busy lady. You're just going to have to wait till she comes on home."

I thought I'd bust open waiting to tell her. When she did come home, I flew out of bed as soon as I woke up and raced up to her room. "Mercedes," I called, knocking on her door. "I've got to talk to you." And when she called for me to come in, I burst into the room.

"He's coming," I said. "He's coming."

"Who's coming?" she said, raising her head from the pillow. "And what time is it?"

"It's almost eight o'clock."

"Eight o'clock?" she said, flopping back down on the pillow. "I've got to get me more sleep."

I ran over to her bed. "But Mercedes," I said, "Elvis is coming. He's coming to town."

She looked up at me, her eyes barely open. "That's nice," she said.

"Nice?" I said. "Is that all you can say, is nice?"

"I'm lucky I can say that much, seeing as it's only eight o'clock in the morning."

"Oh, Mercedes, stop your teasing and listen to me."

"I'm listening," she said, her voice muffled and quiet. "I'm listening."

I sat on the edge of the bed. "Well," I said, "he's going to be at the Dexter Auditorium on September fifth and he's going to be live —"

"I figured that one out, sweetie."

"— and the number to call is 914-555-1000. And the sign said to call fast because the tickets will go."

"Ummmnnn."

"But maybe we won't need tickets," I said. "What do you think?"

"What do I think of what?"

"The tickets," I said. "You think Elvis will want you to buy your own tickets?"

She sat up very slowly, rubbed her eyes, and said, "What did you say?"

"I said, do you think Elvis will want you to buy your own tickets? Tickets. For the show. For you and me."

"How else would we get there?"

"You can call him and ask him for some tickets. I'll bet he'll be happy to do it for you."

"Tell me one good reason why he'd be happy to send me tickets."

"Come on, Mercedes," I said. "He's your friend. You went to school with him. I'd give tickets to my friends."

"Hon," she said, yawning and stretching, "I told you

I went to school with him for exactly two months. I was fifteen years old. Do you think he's going to remember me?"

"But you said you wrote to him and that he wrote back."

"Did I say that?" she said, stretching her arms out.

"Yes, you did, and he *will* remember you. You've got his picture and everything."

She threw the covers to one side and got out of bed. "Well, I see there's going to be no more sleeping for me."

"Get the picture out, Mercedes. Please."

"What picture?" she said, yawning again.

"The picture with Elvis. You said you'd look for it . . ."

"Good Lord," she said, putting on her robe and slippers, "is there no stopping you?" Then she motioned toward the closet and said, "It's in the brown bag."

"Oh, God," I said, when I found it, "it is Elvis." I hugged the picture tight. "It's really him." Then I sat down and really looked at it. "There," I said. "There you are and there he is."

"With forty-two other kids. And the teacher."

I rubbed my hand over the picture. "He'll remember. I'll make him remember."

But Mercedes didn't hear me. She was heading out the door and down the stairs. "Want a cup of coffee?" she called back. "I'm going to have me some coffee."

I ran after her, the picture under my arm. "Do you have his address?" I said.

"Whose address are you talking about?"

"Elvis. Elvis's address."

"Oh, sweetie, why would I have his address?"

"Well, if you don't have it, I'll just send the letter to the Dexter Auditorium. Is it okay if I sign your name?"

She stopped and put her hand on the banister and looked right at me. "Wanda," she said, "Elvis Presley won't remember Mercedes Washington. Nobody remembers Mercedes Washington. I told you, I went to more schools than Elvis has hairs on his head."

But I didn't want to hear what she was saying.

"Wanda," she said slowly, "I can get tickets, same as everybody else. But as far as him sending me tickets, that's just not going to happen."

"He will," I said. "You'll see."

She sighed and started down the stairs. "I really do need to get me a cup of coffee."

My mother was sitting at the kitchen table, reading the supermarket specials. "Chicken's on sale for twenty-three cents a pound, August," she said, "write that on down."

"Chicken," he said, writing it on a piece of paper. "Twenty-three cents a pound."

When Momma saw Mercedes, she reached behind her and got the coffeepot. "Coffee's all ready," she said. "Wanda, get Mercedes a cup?" Then turning to Mercedes, she said, "You sit down now. You must be awfully tired."

Mercedes just smiled.

"The other night was beautiful," my mother said. "I

have never enjoyed myself more. Oh, August, you should have heard her."

My father must have convinced my mother he really was going to stop by now, because she had a kind of soft look on her face. Almost like she used to.

He smiled and said he hoped he'd get to hear her, and Mercedes said he could come anytime.

"Morning, Wanda," my mother said. "Get yourself some milk. Poppa got some doughnuts. You, too, Mercedes, please help yourself."

I was too excited to be hungry, but I didn't want to hurt Poppa's feelings. When he was trying to stop, he always kept busy. He'd walk everywhere, especially to the bakery.

I bit into one and the jelly squirted out onto the tablecloth. "They sure know how to make those jellies," my father said, getting up from the table.

He poured himself some coffee and started out toward the porch. "Wanda," he said, "how about walking down to the shop with me? I sure could use the company."

"Sure, Poppa, whenever you're ready," I said, eating the last piece of doughnut and turning to Mercedes. "Is it okay if I write, seeing as you're so busy, and can I sign your name?"

"Sweetie," she said, "don't waste your time writing to him. I'll get some tickets soon as I get the chance."

"Wanda, stop that pestering and pour Mercedes a cup of coffee," Momma said. "Then let her be."

"I'm not pestering and this is important." Then I

poured Mercedes some coffee and said, "Okay, then, I'll do the writing. You'll see. He'll send us tickets. The best seats in the house."

"Who are you writing to?" my mother asked.

"Elvis. He's coming to town and Mercedes and I are going to see him," I said.

"You just simmer down a minute," my mother said. "I hear he is not what a thirteen-year-old girl should be watching."

"Oh, Momma, I'll die if I don't see him. I'll bet Sarah's seen him already." Then, turning to Mercedes, I said, "Please tell Momma it'll be just fine."

"All the kids love him."

I looked over at my mother. She waited for a minute and then said, "We'll see. Guess it can't do too much harm."

I turned back to Mercedes. "Can I sign your name to the letter?"

Mercedes nodded her head. "Do as you please, hon, but I'll end up buying tickets if you're going to get to see him."

"That's awfully kind of you, Mercedes," Momma said. Then she turned to me and said, "You hush now and let her be. Besides, Poppa must be ready to go. It's getting late."

"Let's take the long way, Wanda," my father said. "George is already there and I need some exercise."

We walked down Marigold Place and on up to Lotus Lane. The morning was bright and clear and the streets had been just cleaned. The road was wet and looked like a long piece of licorice. "Poppa," I said. "Guess who's coming to town?"

He shook his head. "Got no idea."

"Elvis," I said. "He's coming in September. And Mercedes and I are going to go to see him. He'll probably send her front-row tickets."

"That'll be nice," he said, looking up at the sky. "That'll be real nice, Wanda."

"You feeling okay, Poppa?" I said.

He nodded.

"I'm writing to him soon as I get back home."

He nodded again.

"You sure you're okay?"

He looked down at me and put his hand on my shoulder. "It's tough. Especially the first few days. But I'm going to do it. Aren't I, Wanda?"

"Yes, Poppa."

When we got to the shop, he thanked me and gave me a kiss, and as I started out the door, he called out, "Wanda, come on back and walk me home? Will you?"

"Sure, Poppa," I said. "Sure I will."

On the way home, I prayed that Poppa would be there when I got back. And when I didn't want to think about it anymore, I started the letter in my head. "Dear Elvis: What a strange world this is. Here I am in the same town —"

Chapter 13

When I got home from Poppa's shop, I flew up the stairs and headed for my room. Mr. Collins was coming down the hall, dressed in his blue and white summer suit, a book tucked under his arm.

"Morning, Wanda," he said. "Care to join me at Grover's for a bite of breakfast?"

"Thanks, but I just ate," I said, "and I've got a whole lot to do this morning."

"Well, I'd best be on my way," he said, tipping his hat, "because, as Harry Hopkins once said, 'Hunger is not debatable.'"

When I passed his room, his door was opened just a little. He always left it like that. One day he and April May had a big argument about her going into his room when he wasn't there. "You are never, ever to enter this room unless you are invited, Madame," he'd said. She'd told him she'd never done any such thing. "My dear lady," he'd said, "I read Sherlock Holmes and incorporate his methods of catching criminals. The faint footprints on my rug are unmistakably yours."

He'd told me later he had sprinkled an almost invisible layer of talcum powder on his rug. When I'd asked him why he didn't just lock his door, he'd said, with a sad smile, "Old age does strange things to one's mind. I try to keep mine busy even with such foolish things as outwitting April May."

I'd been avoiding April May since the night we went to Savannah. Every time I went past her room she'd call out for me to come in, but I knew if I did, she'd make some nasty remark about Mercedes. Momma told me not to answer her if she did. "That's just what she wants so she can really start up. You just ignore her."

But this morning I couldn't because when I got to the top of the stairs, she was standing in her doorway, Petey in his cage at her feet. "I've been wanting to talk to you," she said. "I want to hear all about Savannah."

"Well," she said, when I got to where she stood, "how was it?"

"I told you. It was wonderful."

"And what about Miss La-De-Da? How was she?"

"She was wonderful, too," I said.

"Watcha doin'? Watcha doin'?"

April May banged Petey's cage and he put his head down and pecked at his perch.

"You'd say that even if she sounded like an old crow," she said, picking up Petey's cage and walking toward me. "Guess your momma don't much care where she goes. Or her daughter either."

"You're just jealous."

"Of who?"

"Of Mercedes."

"And why would I be jealous of the likes of her?"

"Because of all the places she's been and all the people she knows."

"You believe all that stuff she's filling your head with? Well, they're nothing but lies, because that's what folks like Miss La-De-Da Washington do. Why, she even came into this house lying."

"What are you talking about?"

"She had to lie 'cause no respectable house takes her kind. She's nothing but a nigger girl."

I felt like April May had slapped me. "That's a terrible thing to say."

"Terrible or not, it's true. I seen it for myself. She's got pictures of herself with colored. Lots of colored."

"You did it again, didn't you? You spied . . ."

April May dropped Petey's cage, grabbed me by the arm, pulled me into her room, and closed the door.

"You shut your mouth," she hissed.

"No," I said. "I'm going to tell Momma this time."

She yanked my arm and said, "You tell your momma and I'll tell everybody in this house and everybody else I know that your momma's got a nigger living up in her attic . . ."

Her eyes narrowed. "You know you can be arrested for having colored in the same boardinghouse as whites? You know that? And she is as colored as I am white."

I wanted to hit her. "You're lying."

"It ain't me that's lying. Ask her. I dare you. I can tell you now, she won't tell you nothing, 'cause she's afraid she'll get her walking papers, too."

"Hello. Hello . . ."

"And if you think Elvis what's his name is going to remember her, you've got another think coming." She banged Petey's cage again. "Ain't that right, Petey boy?" Her eyes were slits. She bent down and said in a low voice, "Don't you know niggers don't go to school with white folk?"

"I wish you'd never come to this house," I said. "The only reason you're here is because no one else wants you."

"I pay my way," she said. "And don't you forget it, girl."

Then she pushed me back out into the hall and closed the door.

I banged the door with my fist and said, "Just you wait. You're wrong. She's not the one who's lying. And he *will* remember her. You'll see."

"What's going on up there?" my mother called from downstairs.

"Nothing, Momma."

"Well, it doesn't sound like nothing."

My legs shook as I walked down to my room. I flung myself down on the bed, pulled the bear close, and even though I didn't want to cry, I did.

— *April May is so hateful. And she's wrong. She's lying. Making up those stories about Mercedes. It can't be true. She* did *go to school with Elvis. I saw the picture myself. Oh, God, I wish Sarah were here.*

I turned and looked over at Elvis. "You will remember her, won't you? It's not fair if you don't. She remembers everything about you and you weren't famous then."

— He has to. He just has to. Because if he doesn't, April May will never shut up and Mercedes might leave and I couldn't stand . . . I've got to talk to Poppa. He'll fix April May.

I wiped my face and ran down the stairs and onto the porch. My mother was leaning against the porch rail, a glass in her hand. "Just cooling off," she said. "Want some ice tea?"

I shook my head. "You need anything down at Flitty's?" I said. "I'm going down to see Poppa for a while."

"He's not there. He called and said he and George had to put in a cooling unit for a new customer."

"But he asked me to come on back to walk him home at suppertime."

"Well, it's not suppertime," she said. "Besides, he said to tell you he'd most likely be late finishing up and probably would go straight to a meeting."

She held the glass to her forehead. "The heat's really bothering me today. You sure you don't want some tea? Fresh made."

"No thanks, Momma." I went back into the house, letting the screen door slam behind me. I walked up the stairs one at a time, thinking about all the terrible things April May had said, and my stomach knotted.

— *Just when everything seemed to be going along fine, April May's got to cause trouble. What does she have against Mercedes? Mercedes is good and she's kind. Even Momma seems different with Mercedes being here. Poppa, too.*

When I got back to my room, I put Elvis on the record player. I swayed in time to the music and when Elvis sang *"Ain't that lovin' you, baby,"* I hummed along with him. And when he stopped singing, I stood looking at his picture for a long time. Then I turned the record over, got a pen and paper, and started to write.

Dear Elvis:

It's such a small world, isn't it. Imagine me singing in the same town as you're appearing . . .

— *This is stupid. Maybe I should tell him about the time they were in school together. That'll remind him —*

Dear Elvis:

I'm hoping you'll remember me. We were in Miss Fitzhugh's class at Humes High School. I was the girl who came in kind of late in the year . . .

— *I wish Sarah were here to help me with this. She'd be better at it than I am.*

Dear Elvis:

— If I were writing to him from me I'd know what to say. I'd tell him how every girl in school loves him. I'd tell him how I got to like him when Sarah gave me his record when she came home from Memphis. And that now I love him. And how I've never been there or anywhere, except for Savannah. And how when Momma and Poppa argue or when I get scared about Poppa's drinking, I put him on the record player and he makes me feel safe. And then I'd tell him I know everything about him. Well, almost everything. I'd tell him I know his middle name is Aron. And how much he loves his mother. And then I'd tell him I know about his twin brother dying right when he was born and how sorry I am about that. I might even tell him about the new baby coming and how I want to feel good about it but sometimes I just feel kind of scared about how I might have to take care of it. And how sometimes I get scared that Poppa might drink again even though I want to believe he won't. He'd know what to tell me. He'd tell me it was okay to feel that way —

I scrunched up about a hundred letters and walked around my room about a thousand times before I finally wrote one that didn't sound completely stupid.

Dear Elvis:

Imagine my surprise when I saw the poster announcing your visit to Savannah. I am just thrilled. I'm singing at Le Jazz every evening, except Sunday, and would just love it if you came on over to see me. I can arrange to have a table set up for you — for two, or ten, or twenty. Just let me know.

I've been telling a friend of mine (who just happens to be your biggest fan) all about you, and Memphis, and Miss Fitzhugh. Wanda, that's her name, Wanda Sue Dohr is very anxious to meet you, in fact, she can hardly wait.

Well, I'd best get ready for my gig and I'll anxiously await to hear from you.

Love,
Mercedes Washington

I kept reading the letter over and over. Then I signed Mercedes's name, and when I heard April May call to the mailman, "Hey, Sam, anything for me today?" I sealed it up and raced down to hand it to him. I asked him when he thought it would be delivered.

He glanced at the envelope. "Day or two at most."

"Waste of time taking that one," April May called out.

Sam didn't answer her; he just told me to have myself a fine day, tucked the letter in his bag, and walked on down the path.

Chapter 14

I'd tried to wait up for Poppa, but I couldn't stay awake. Mercedes got home late and I heard her tell Momma she was leaving early this morning for another rehearsal. I jumped out of bed, pulled my robe around me, and ran down to the kitchen. Momma was in her gardening clothes.

"Morning," she said. "You sleep well?"

I nodded. But I hadn't. I kept dreaming. Scary ones about April May. I dreamt that her head came out of a keyhole, tiny at first, and then bigger and bigger until her face filled the doorway. Then the hall. And then the whole house, squeezing out all of us. "Where's Poppa?" I said. "I wanted to walk with him."

"He left early. Something came up down at the shop."

"I'm going down to see him."

"He's not there yet. Said he'd be there about two."

"You sure he's not there now?"

"He was going on by Miz Love's," she said, handing me a glass of juice. "Do me a favor when you do go.

Pick up the picture at Mr. Trask's. It ought to be ready now. I've got a ton of things I want to get done today," she said. Then she smoothed her smock over her stomach and smiled. "I'm beginning to show."

"Show what?"

"That I'm going to have a baby."

"I don't notice anything different," I said, helping myself to cereal.

"Well, my clothes are tight. When I carried you, I didn't show until I was almost ready to deliver."

I didn't want to talk about it. I didn't even know if she'd told Poppa yet. The one time I'd asked her, she told me she'd do it in due time.

She poured herself some coffee and started toward the door. "When you're finished, could you help me stake the tomatoes?"

"Sure, Momma."

Momma was changing a little. She wasn't telling me every minute to do this and that. Like this morning, letting me sleep a little late and asking me to help her instead of telling me. And even though she got the crazies about Poppa sometimes, she was trying with him, too.

We worked till noon and when the last tomato plant was staked, I went into the house and took a long bath. I brought a pad and pencil into the tub with me and started a letter to Sarah.

Dear Sarah:

How's California? I miss you. I wish you were home

so I could tell you all about what's going on here instead of having to write about it. We've got a new boarder. You'd like her. She's beautiful, really beautiful, and she's a singer. I got to hear her sing in Savannah and had supper at her club. But that's not the most exciting thing that's happening here. I'm going to see Elvis. Yes, the *Elvis. Our Elvis. Mercedes (that's her name) went to school with him —*

"Other people have got to use the bathroom," April May yelled, banging on the door.

I didn't answer her, but she kept banging and calling.

"There's one in the basement," I said.

"I ain't using that one, so hurry up."

April May just came to the door. She is getting meaner than ever. Poppa is going to try to get her married to Mr. Murphy. Poor Mr. Murphy. He doesn't deserve that.

April May banged again.

Anyway, as I was telling you, Mercedes knows Elvis. She told me all about him. She wrote to him (well, I wrote to him but she told me it was all right) and asked him to send tickets — Sarah, when are you coming home? Wouldn't it be something if you got to go, too? —

"I'm calling your mother," April May said, banging on the door harder. "You got no right hogging the facilities away from paying renters."

It was no use. I knew she'd never stop. I finished the letter to Sarah and got out of the tub.

"I'm out," I called out when I passed her room. "And if you take a bath, I won't be here to help you out."

I got dressed quickly and went to the post office to mail the letter. As it slid down the chute, I realized I hadn't told Sarah about the baby. I watched the letter fall into the box behind the counter; then I turned and ran all the way to Poppa's shop. When I got there the shop was quiet.

"Poppa," I called.

No answer.

"Poppa," I called again. Louder.

I ran through the shop and out the back door and into the storage yard. "Poppa," I yelled.

"Over here," he said.

I took a deep breath and whispered, "Oh, God, thank you."

He and Mr. Gingrich were lifting a sink onto the truck.

"For Miz Love's new bathroom," Poppa said.

They got the sink into the truck and then my father climbed in and gently eased it into the back of the truck.

"How you doing, Wanda?" Mr. Gingrich said, pulling his hat from his head and wiping his forehead with his sleeve. "Hot enough for you?"

"Sort of. But I like it."

When the sink was finally settled, my father stood in the middle of the truck, put his arms behind his neck and rubbed it. "This is the third sink we've delivered to her," he said. "You absolutely sure this is the right one, George? The one she picked out herself?"

"I am."

"Well, it better be. My back is killing me."

"Then let's call it a day, Aug," Mr. Gingrich said. "My back's none too good either and Miz Love's not expecting this till Monday."

My father hopped from the truck, chewing on a candy bar. "Have some," he said.

I shook my head. When Poppa wasn't drinking, he loved candy and all that stuff. Momma couldn't understand it but Mercedes told me that's why he bought doughnuts when he wasn't drinking. "Got to replace the drink with something," she'd said, "and sugar's it."

Poppa went in to wash up, and I ran over to Mr. Trask's and got the picture, making sure he put the bill in the package. When I got back to Poppa's shop, Mr. Gingrich was leaving.

"Come on," my father said, locking the front door. "Let's go down to Grover's and get us some ice cream. Care to come, George?"

Mr. Gingrich said he was much obliged to be asked but he had to stop by the hardware store to pick up his fan. "And then I'll go right on home," he said. "Want to make sure the fan is fixed proper. Thought I'd die of the heat last night."

"Come on, then," my father said, putting his arm around me. "Let's get us some lemonade, too. I've got an awful thirst."

We sat at a table by the window at Grover's and ate ice cream and drank lemonade. I wanted to tell Poppa about April May, but Mr. Grover had a reputation for listening to everybody's conversations and so I decided to wait.

It was good to be with Poppa. He was friendly to everybody. He didn't even take offense when Mr. Grover said how unusual it was to see Poppa drinking lemonade and eating ice cream. Momma would have made a fuss and said she knew what Mr. Grover was getting at and how she'd never come back into his store again. But not Poppa. He just kept drinking and licking and when we were through, he told Mr. Grover he had just about the best lemonade in the state of Georgia, and then we were on our way.

"See you again, August," Mr. Grover said, with some sincerity.

"Sure thing," my father said.

Poppa wanted to take the long way and that was all right with me. I couldn't wait to tell him what April May said about Mercedes. But before I could, he said he had something serious to tell me. He told me about Momma having a baby, like he didn't know I knew. So I pretended I didn't. I didn't want him to know I'd known about it before he did. I acted real surprised. And happy, too. But I still felt scared about it.

"Sure came as a surprise to me," he said. "Thought

Momma didn't want one now that she thinks you're almost grown. But she's thought that for a long time, hasn't she, Wanda?"

I shrugged. But I knew what he was saying.

"It's true," he said, taking the package from my hand and putting it under his arm. "Momma thinks you're older and wiser than both of us. And you know what? She's right. Not that I'm saying it's right she thinks that way. I'm just saying that's the way you are."

That was just like Poppa. He said things just right. When Momma said how grown up I was, I hated it because what she meant was that I could do a million things around the house. But when Poppa said it, it was different.

The air was still and the sun was hot, and when we came to the bench in front of Town Hall, I asked Poppa if we could sit down. "Sure thing," he said.

"Poppa," I said, "I've got something I've got to tell you."

He put his arm around me. "What is it? Are you all right?"

I nodded. "It's about April May."

"What's she done now?"

"She said a terrible thing about Mercedes."

"What?"

"She called her an awful name."

"She's good at that. I'll give her a talking-to."

"It was worse this time," I said. "You know what she called her?"

He shook his head.

"A ni —" The word stuck in my throat. "She called her a ni — . . . a nigger girl," I said finally, spitting the words from my mouth.

Poppa shook his head and frowned. He didn't say anything for a while. Then he sighed and said, "That is an ugly word. And one that I won't permit in my home."

"Don't tell Momma I told you, but April May went into Mercedes's room. She said she saw pictures of Mercedes with colored people. And she said Mercedes lied about herself because respectable people wouldn't take in her kind."

"She has really crossed the line this time. April May's got no right to butt in to someone else's business, and . . ."

Poppa was missing the point. "But she's *lying.* I know she is. Mercedes went to school with Elvis. I saw the picture."

He looked straight at me, a serious look on his face.

"Wanda, honey," he said gently. "April May said some mean things, but I don't think she's lying about Mercedes being colored."

I was confused. "She can't be . . ."

"Does it matter if she is?"

"But she would have told me."

"Does it matter, honey?" he asked again.

I shrugged. I didn't know what to think. Most of all, I was thinking that Mercedes and I were friends. Best friends. "She should have told me," I said. I got up and walked slowly to the curb and sat down. My father followed. After a while, I turned to him and said, "Does it matter to you?"

He shook his head slowly. "It doesn't matter to me," he said. "And if it ever had mattered, all I have to do is look at you and what she's come to mean to you in the short time she's been here."

"If it is true, what about Momma? You know how she worries about what people think. What if April May starts trouble?"

He put his hand against my cheek. "Your Momma knows. She knew for sure the night you all went to Savannah."

I tried to think what happened that night that would've told her, but I couldn't remember anything right now.

"Does Mercedes know you know?"

He nodded.

"What's Momma going to do? I don't want Mercedes to leave. But April May says Momma could get arrested. And I know her. Even if I don't tell Momma she went into Mercedes's room, she'll tell everybody and then maybe Mercedes will have to . . ."

"You leave April May to me." Then he looked straight at me. "Don't you sell your momma short. She seems like she's hard sometimes, but that doesn't mean her heart isn't still as soft as it always was. And besides, she's fond of Mercedes. Very fond of her. I know that. So do you."

He shook his head again. "I don't understand April

May. She's my own sister and I don't know what makes her like she is. I truly don't. Our folks were ignorant in lots of ways, but they didn't judge people by the color the Lord gave them. But April May, now she's a different story. Sometimes she can be as ugly as that word she used. But I am still head of my home and I intend to tell her just that."

"Poppa," I said, "do you think I should tell Mercedes that I know?"

"I think one of these days it'll come out just as natural as the sun comes up every morning."

He put his arm around me and pulled me close. "Things are going to work out. I can handle April May. You'll see."

Then he went back to the bench and picked up the picture. He sat for a while, the picture on his lap, and then he motioned for me to come sit next to him.

And when I did, he hugged me and said, "Let's see what kind of a job Trask did."

When he got it opened, I couldn't see the part that was slit. But I knew it was there. The slit between Momma and Poppa.

"Look how handsome you are, Poppa," I said.

"I was kind of handsome, wasn't I?" he said. "And look at your mother." He looked over at me. "God, you look like her. Beautiful."

He rubbed his elbow against the glass and looked again. "I don't remember ever being that young."

"You're still young, Poppa."

"I don't feel it." Then he looked down at his work clothes and said, "Never thought I'd follow in my poppa's business. Always thought I'd do something more."

"What would you do if you could, Poppa?"

"Study the stars. Always was fascinated by them. But my pa thought that was for fools. I think I would have been good at that. Teaching it maybe. I like kids." He gave me a quick squeeze.

"It's not too late," I said. "Plenty of people do it later. Like Sarah's father. She told me she was eight years old when he graduated school."

"I know, but that was different. Now, I'm not making excuses, but can you see me starting back to school with you getting ready to go to college soon and a new baby coming?"

"Babies grow up," I said.

He turned to me. "You sound like you ought to be my mother instead of my daughter. You've got more common sense than I do." He looked away and then said, "I ought to get me to another AA meeting tonight. There's one down at the Grange, I think."

Sometimes Momma hated it when Poppa went to meetings. When he was drinking she'd tell him he ought to go, and then when he did she'd tell him it wasn't a good idea to bring any of "those people" home.

"That's a fine idea, Poppa."

He hugged me again. "I didn't ask you what you want to be," he said. "You'll be through high school before you know it."

"Maybe a teacher, too," I said. "But I want to go away to school. I don't want to stay in Harmony the way Momma did."

"I won't hold you back, Wanda." He put the picture back in the paper, wrapping it very carefully. "I promise you."

We started for home again, walking slowly, not talking. When we passed Mr. Murphy's street, I thought about April May again and how good it would be if she'd go away.

"Poppa," I said, "do you think Mr. Murphy's ship is ever going to come in?"

"It sure doesn't look that way," he said.

"Do you think Mr. Murphy really loves April May?"

"I think he does," he said, shaking his head. "A fact I cannot figure out."

"I think so, too, because she once told me he's very jealous," I said. "She told me when they were picnicking one day, the mailman told her how cool she looked sitting under the shade tree. She said Mr. Murphy got so mad his face turned purple."

"Really?"

"Yep. She said he told Sam to stop gawking at his intended."

"Didn't think Henry was the jealous type."

Poppa stopped walking, stood still for a few seconds, then kissed me and said, "Wanda, my love, you are a genius. You have given me an idea." He glanced down at his watch. "Come on, we've got just enough time before supper to pay Mr. Henry Murphy a visit."

"What did I say?"

Poppa didn't answer me. He smoothed the wrapping on the package, took my arm, and started down toward Mr. Murphy's house. His face glowed. Sometimes he'd get very excited about things. Wound up, my mother would say. And then sometimes, just as quick, he'd get all down about things. Depressed. And that's when things would go bad.

"What did I say?" I asked again.

"That Henry Murphy is a very jealous man."

"So what's that going to do?"

"We are going to make him more jealous."

"How?"

"You just said he was jealous of Sam, didn't you?"

"Yes, but . . ."

"That's our answer, hon. We make Henry think April May's got a boyfriend."

"But she doesn't."

"So we fib. They love each other, don't they?" He looked up at the sky and said, "You do work in strange ways, don't you, Lord."

When we got to Mr. Murphy's driveway, I could see him sitting on the porch, holding a glass.

"Well, now, Henry," my father said, sauntering up the front walk, "fancy seeing you here."

"This is home."

"Wanda and I are heading down to the post office." He looked at his watch, then over at me. "Better watch our time, else they'll be closing. And you know what April May said. 'Get that package down before they close. I promised Lloyd Gibbons he'd have these cookies by Tuesday at the latest.'"

Mr. Murphy put his glass down and stood up. "Who's Lloyd Gibbons and why's April May sending him cookies?"

"April May'd have my hide if she knew I let the cat out of the bag."

"What cat out of what bag?"

"Well, you know, April May's an attractive lady, leastways I think she is. Don't you think so, Wanda?"

"Yes, Poppa."

"Well, it appears some old beau from Claxton thinks so too. Been writing to her . . ."

"She never told me that."

"That's 'cause she's so sweet on you, isn't she, Wanda?"

"She sure is," I said.

"Why, I know for a fact my sister would like nothing better than to be April May Murphy."

I started to laugh, but Poppa poked me.

"Well, we don't want to rush into that . . ."

"Oh, listen, Henry, I understand. Men do. But you know how women are. Wanting to tie that knot. Right, Wanda?"

"They sure do, Poppa."

— If Momma were here, she'd kill us. But it isn't as if Poppa is hurting anybody. He's helping. Helping all of us.

Mr. Murphy leaned against the porch rail and shook his head back and forth. "I can't understand this. Why,

April May and me have been promised to one another for going on four years now . . ."

"Four years is a long time for a woman to wait. Right, Wanda?"

"Right, Poppa."

Mr. Murphy sat on the porch rail, still shaking his head back and forth. "I can't let that sweet little lady get away."

"We know just how you feel, Henry. Don't we, Wanda?"

"We sure do."

My father winked at me and handed me the package. "Better run this on down to the post office. Don't want to miss the last mail. April May'll have our heads if we do."

"Wait a minute," Mr. Murphy said. "You just hold on a minute. That Lloyd what's his name can wait. I've got to do me some thinking."

"Fair enough," my father said. "But better do it fast, Henry. Time waits for no man."

Poppa took my arm and we started down the walk.

"You tell April May I'll be over soon as I change my shirt," Mr. Murphy called. "You tell her that, you hear?"

"We hear you," Poppa said as he strutted down the walk, me strutting beside him. "Don't we, Wanda?"

"We sure do, Poppa," I said. "We surely do."

Chapter 15

I swear Poppa and I weren't home an hour when Mr. Murphy appeared all dressed up to ask my father for April May's hand in marriage. My father rushed from the kitchen, telling Momma to stay put. Then Poppa ushered Mr. Murphy into the parlor, said a quick "Yes Sirree," and then excused himself.

"I won't be long, Henry," he said. "Got to see April May about something. Wanda, see that Momma fixes Mr. Murphy a cool drink."

Then Poppa went upstairs and as I walked through the hall, I heard him knock on April May's door. Hard. "April May," he said in a tone of voice I'd never heard before. "It's your brother and I've got something to say to you. And you'd best listen to me carefully. Very carefully."

I wished I were a flea in Petey's feathers so I could hear what he was saying to her. I went into the kitchen and asked Momma what she wanted to give Mr. Murphy.

"April May," she whispered, her hand over her mouth to stop laughing.

"Momma," I said, "did Poppa tell you what I told him about April May and Mercedes?"

She nodded. "You know what? It's so strange the way I feel about Mercedes. I keep telling myself I hardly know her, but I feel I've known her forever." She smiled, but not really at me. "She's the first person I've ever felt close to outside of you and Poppa." Then she turned and busied herself fixing Mr. Murphy's ginger tea.

I went over and slipped my arms around her waist. She squeezed my hands quickly. "Come on, now, we've got a guest in our parlor." She turned and gave me the tea.

I started for the parlor, but April May was coming down the stairs, calling to Mr. Murphy. She looked like she'd been crying.

He came to the bottom of the stairs and when he saw her, he held out his hand. April May stood as still as a willow on a windless morning. Then she smiled and nodded her head. So did Mr. Murphy, and, without a word passing between them, he took her hand and led her to the car.

Poppa came down after a while. He nodded to Momma and me. "Ladies, April May won't be causing any more trouble," he said, a smile creeping over his face. "Mind you, now, she doesn't agree with what I've had to say, but April May's no fool. I reminded her that her intended's family might look poorly on her if she was asked to leave my home before the wedding. 'April May,' I said, 'some folks think it's rather disgraceful for respectable Southern ladies not to be given in marriage by kin from their own home. And since I am your only kin, you'd best act like a respectable Southern lady till the two of us walk down that aisle.'"

Chapter 16

"I do not understand what all this hurry is about," my mother said. "Henry has put off getting married to April May for years. And now, a few days after he proposes, he wants to get married in a matter of weeks."

She opened the oven and basted the ham. "I truly do not understand that at all."

"Don't question things so much, Jane Ann," Poppa said.

"You want baked sweet potato or white?" she asked.

"Both," he said.

"You, Wanda?"

"Sweet, Momma," I said. "Did I get any mail today?"

"Can't say that I saw any."

"I thought I'd hear by now, but I guess he's awfully busy what with movies and records," I said to no one in particular.

I missed not seeing Mercedes. She'd stayed in town

for a couple of days. "Got to rehearse with a new group," she'd told my mother. But today she was coming home early and I wanted to talk to her. Poppa had said that talking to Mercedes about her being colored would come out as natural as the sun. And that's what I wanted. I didn't want it to be like a secret that I was holding on to. I didn't like secrets. They were like shadows, keeping people from the light.

My mother took the ham out of the oven and put it on the table.

"Well, I'd better get busy and plan something," she said, rubbing her back. "You remember what you promised your mother, August."

He nodded his head. "Could be worse. April May could have been twins, but life is not all *that* cruel."

"Don't put so much of that sweet sauce on your ham, August. Too much isn't good for you."

She passed the rolls to me and motioned for me to pass them to my father, smoothing the tablecloth as she spoke. "I can't say I'm too happy about having to entertain all the Murphys. Especially Odell. She's about the nastiest young woman I've ever met, and Calhoun's no bargain either."

My father didn't answer her; he just kept eating.

"August," she said, "you tell them there'll be absolutely no liquor brought into this house. You'll have to come right out in the open and tell them, otherwise I can see it happening. Henry likes his drink and so does Calhoun and I've heard that Mrs. Murphy likes a nip or two."

My father finished his supper and poured himself a cup of coffee. "I'm going down to the Grange tonight, Jane Ann."

"Again?" she said and then she stopped. She looked over at me. "Why don't you walk down with Poppa?"

Whenever I thought Momma was really changing, she'd start up again worrying about Poppa's drinking, and he was trying so hard. Mercedes told me that Momma would come around in time. "She's just scared he'll go off again."

My father sighed and looked over at her and said, "Jane Ann, Wanda's not my keeper." He put three spoons of sugar in his coffee and said, "I'll be all right. Maybe I'll call somebody to walk on down with."

"Meet at the corner," she said.

He nodded his head. "I'll do that, Jane Ann, if that's what you want."

"Well, I was only thinking that it'd save time." She got up from the table and started to fix April May's plate. "We've got to plan what we're going to serve, August. Weddings aren't cheap. Do you suppose Mr. Murphy might help?"

But my father didn't hear her. He had taken his coffee out to the porch and was sitting on the glider. I went out after him and we sat swinging until it was time for him to leave. "I'll come with you, Poppa, if you want."

"No need. But thank you kindly." He called in a good-bye to my mother and she called back a good-night and then she said, "Make sure you lock up when you come in, August, and come right on up to bed."

It was always the same with Momma when Poppa went to AA. "What kind of people are there?" she asked the first time Poppa went.

"Folks with four legs and six heads and an eye in the middle of their nose," Poppa had said, hoping to make her laugh. But she hadn't. She'd told me to go up to bed so she could discuss something with Poppa. I listened from the stairs and I could hear her telling him that it wasn't a good idea to bring any of them home. "After all, we've got Wanda to think of."

That puzzled me, because Poppa was one of "them." I tried to tell her that one day, but she told me to hush up, that I'd understand what it was all about when I grew up. That was another thing about Momma that drove me crazy. When she wanted me to do something, she'd treat me like I was forty years old, but when she didn't want me to do something, she told me I'd be able to do it when I grew up.

"Wanda," my mother called, "will you take April May's tray up before she starts banging?"

I walked back to the kitchen slowly and took the tray in my hands. "Momma," I said, "why can't you trust Poppa?"

"What a thing to say."

"It's true, Momma. And he's trying so hard."

She brushed her hair back and looked at me. "He always does," she said, "but that doesn't mean he's going to make it."

"He *is* going to make it," I said. "You'll see."

"I hope so. I'm tired of living this way. Uncertain of what's going to happen."

She sat down at the kitchen table and for a minute I thought she was going to cry. "I love Poppa," she said. "I really do."

"Then you've got to let him know you trust him. Mercedes said that's important."

"I know . . ."

"He's got to know you believe in him. Everybody needs someone to believe in them, Momma."

"I do in my heart, but then sometimes my head gets in the way." She picked up the place mats and wiped them down. Then she rubbed her back and sighed. For the first time, I could see Momma's stomach bulging out.

"You feeling all right?"

"Just a little stiff," she said. "You go on up now. April May's been waiting awhile now."

"Hello. Hello," Petey called when I knocked on April May's door. I hated going in there, even though April May hadn't said anything else since Poppa had talked to her.

"Hello, Petey."

"Watcha doin'? Watcha doin'?"

"About time," April May said. "I'm starving." Then she motioned for me to sit down. "I've got something I want to ask you."

I didn't want to sit down. Ever since she came to live here I never wanted to visit with her. Sometimes I'd help her clean Petey's cage so he wouldn't have to spend so much time in the shoe box, or I'd persuade April May to let me clean the cage in the bathroom. I'd drag the cage into the bathroom and let Petey out to fly around for a while.

April May pulled a towel from the windowsill and put it under her chin and tucked the end of it onto her lap. "Murph's picking me up in a little while. We're going over to Odell's house for coffee and cake. Seems like the family wants to get to know me better."

I smiled and said that was very nice.

"I don't much like her," she said. "And I sure don't like her kids."

And I didn't like April May. "What did you want to ask me?"

"Well, you are my niece," she said, stuffing a piece of ham into her mouth, "and I am getting married."

"I know."

"Murph is something, ain't he? Once he makes up his mind, nothing's going to stop him."

"What did you want to ask me?" I asked again.

"Well, I was thinking it'd be nice to have you as my attendant. I told you I don't much like Odell, and before Murph gets it into his head that I ought to ask her, I thought I better ask one of my own. You are blood, you know."

I began to shift my feet around.

"So it's settled," she said. "You are my official attendant."

"I don't have anything to wear."

"Oh, yes, you do," she said. "You know the dress that Miss La-De-Da gave you? You can wear that one. Your momma said she was going to make mine. Things are happening so fast, I'm losing my breath." She slathered butter on a roll and shoved it into her mouth.

I really didn't want to be her official attendant, and I hated it when she called Mercedes "Miss La-De-Da," but I didn't say anything. And besides, when Momma told Poppa six weeks was too soon to plan a wedding, he had said, "Let's not do anything to interrupt the flow of this wedding."

"When you're finished, call me, and I'll take the tray down," I said.

When I started toward the door, Petey called out, "Hello. Hello."

"Good-bye. You say good-bye when somebody's leaving."

"Your momma said Petey could stay here till I get settled. Don't you let him out of his cage. He wouldn't know how to get along without me."

"But I will," I said under my breath and went down to the hall to my room to wait for Mercedes.

I put Elvis on, but I didn't feel like dancing or anything. I was beginning to get really nervous about not hearing from him. I checked the mailbox a million times a day but nothing was ever for me. Mercedes said she told me so, but I knew he'd answer me. He had to. He just had to.

Chapter 17

When it got to be time for Mercedes to come home, I went out to the porch and sat on the glider.

A soft afternoon rain began to fall. It splashed on the honeysuckle and after a while it dripped from the roof onto the railing. One drop after another. Drip. Drip. Drip. I counted them, and when I got to a hundred and two drips, Mercedes's car pulled into the driveway. She got out, and just as she did, it began to rain hard. She let out a little yell and ran around to the trunk and took out a shopping bag.

"Hi, there, sweet thing," she called. "Have I ever got something gooooood in this bag."

She ran up the walk and up the porch steps, clutching the bag to her chest. Her hair was wet and drops ran down her face. She leaned over me and shook her head. "Why should you be sitting there all nice and dry with me looking like a wet hound dog?" She laughed and looked down at me. "You look so serious, hon. You feeling all right?"

I didn't answer her.

"Something troubling you?"

I shrugged.

"Come on upstairs. We'll talk. And eat. I've got some gooey chocolate in this bag waiting for somebody like you and me."

When we got to her room, she took her shoes off and threw them in the corner. She wrapped a towel around her hair, put her robe on, and sat in the rocker. She motioned for me to sit on the floor next to her. Then she pulled out a big box of chocolates from the shopping bag and handed it to me. I picked out two pieces and gave it back to her. She studied the box, shaking her head, touching first one piece and then another.

"Always had trouble making decisions," she said, popping one piece in her mouth and taking out another before handing the box back to me. "Help yourself." She settled herself back in the rocker. "And now can you tell me why we're taking so long to get to what we're going to talk about? And just what are we going to talk about?"

I took a deep breath, waited a long minute, and then said, "Well, the other day Poppa and I had this conversation."

She nodded.

"Anyway, it was the day Mr. Murphy asked April May to marry him —"

"I am one sorry lady to have missed that day."

". . . the day after I mailed the letter to Elvis."

"Oh, hon, you still thinking you're going to hear from him."

"I will."

She shrugged. "Okay. Okay. Sorry I interrupted you."

"— anyway, you know how mean April May is . . ."

"I do. I surely do."

"Well, I told Poppa she said some terrible things about you."

"What she call me this time? Miss La-De-Da Nothing or 'that little tart'?"

I shook my head.

She looked at me for a long time and then nodded with her whole body; the towel slipped from her head. "Aaah," she said. "I think I know. In fact, I know I know. Old April May told you I wasn't as white as I appear. That's what she told you? Not in those words, but that's what she said."

"Yes," I whispered.

"Well, I suppose your poppa told you she was right."

I nodded.

"Nothing wrong with it, is there? Or is there?"

"Not with me, Mercedes. But I didn't know. You didn't tell me . . ."

"And if I had, what difference would it have made?"

"No dif —" But she didn't let me finish.

"Do people have to declare what they are? Do white people? They sure don't." She leaned toward me. "Should I have come into this house saying, 'You know, all you white folks, I want you to know I am part Negro.

Oh, God, you get up from the floor now. And you, over there, fan that lady who just fainted.'" She got up from the rocker.

"Or should folks like me put a sign on our arm, like the black band some folks wear when they just lost someone? Better have that black band on your arm, else folks won't know how much you're hurting inside. Your face won't tell them, just that black arm band. Is that what white people want us to do?"

"No, Mercedes," I said, my voice cracking. 'No. I . . ."

"Oh, sweetie, I'm not talking about you," she said. "And not your poppa or your momma. It's been different here for me. You folks live in a kind of vacuum. You've never seen what I've seen. You want to know how many rooms I'd looked at before I called your momma? Dark, dingy holes." She stopped and laughed out loud. "Last one I tried told me he wouldn't rent to a white woman. Can you believe that one?"

But before I could answer her, she started talking again. "When I picked up the *Harmony Times* and saw your momma's ad, I called her. Now she didn't say, 'Miz Washington, what color are your eyes and what color is your hair and what color is your skin?' She just told me the rent would be thirteen-fifty every other week, gave me the directions, and here I am."

Mercedes paced up and down as fast as she was talking. "Should I have said to her, 'Hold on there, Miz Dohr, I can pay thirteen-fifty and I am a tidy lady and I won't be a bother to you, but I've got to tell you one thing, I'm colored'? My momma was white and my real daddy was colored. Should I have told her I never knew my real daddy 'cause he died when I was two? Should I have told her he was an educated man who had to take a job as a school janitor when he should have been teaching there?"

She stopped talking and went over to the window and looked out. The rain was still falling, spattering on the glass and sliding off the branches of the willow tree.

Without turning, she said, "I'm tired of all this. Tired of figuring out do I tell, don't I tell, what'll I tell, when do I tell." She leaned her forehead against the window. "Only time I truly denied being what I am was when I went to Humes. I wanted that so bad, I used my stepdaddy's name. I told them I was Mercedes McIver." She laughed a little. "He was white, my stepdaddy."

I wanted to say something, but I didn't know what.

After a while, she came over and sat in the rocker. "I'm talking too much," she said. "Have a chocolate."

I shook my head.

Mercedes sat perfectly still, looking straight ahead. "You know what I want?" she said, picking up one of the chocolates. "I want to just be. Looking the way I do, I'm neither here nor there. Not white. Not colored. But I am still me."

She put the chocolate to her lips. "Did you know there's such a thing as white chocolate?" she said. "Oh, for sure it doesn't look the same. Some folks think it's unnatural-looking. But you know what?" And before I could answer her, she popped the chocolate in her mouth, rocked back and forth, and said, "It's just as sweet."

"I'm glad you came here," I said.

"I know. I know," she said, resting her hand on mine. "And for sure I am, too. And you know what, I have talked too much. All this has been stuffed inside me for so long, I've talked myself out." She sighed and looked beyond me toward the window, as though she were alone in another place.

I thought about what Momma had told me about Mercedes not being able to sit at the table with us that night we went to Savannah. She sang so good and everybody clapped and wanted more, but still she couldn't have supper with us. Just because she was colored.

Tears came to my eyes. My throat was tight.

"Well, now, sweetie, I am one tired lady. Too much talking." She laughed. "And I've got to sparkle again tonight."

She got up and put her arm around me. "Now, you remember what I said. I'm still me. Still Mercedes Washington."

I nodded.

"I do something you don't like, you tell me. Same as I'll do for you. Right?"

I nodded again, not trusting my voice.

I walked down the stairs very slowly and went into my room. I closed the door behind me and sat on my bed. Tears slid down my cheeks.

— Why does it have to be like this for her? It's not fair.

Elvis smiled over at me. "You'd better remember her," I said. "She deserves to have you remember her." I reached over and put my record on and stretched out on my bed and listened.

"*. . . makes no difference where I go, or what I do, you know I'll always be loving you . . .*"

And when Elvis stopped singing, I remembered something Mercedes had said. I looked over at him and said, "That's why you didn't answer. She didn't use her right name."

I started toward the door.

— No. No. I'm not going to tell her. I'll just write and tell him she was Mercedes McIver then.

I found some paper and wrote as fast as I could. And when I finished, I tore down the stairs and out the door. I didn't stop running until I dropped the letter in the chute at the post office.

"Now you'll remember," I said.

Chapter 18

Ever since Mr. Murphy proposed to April May, the days had been flying by. Momma was busy sewing April May's gown and planning the wedding breakfast, and Poppa was working hard at the shop. Even though Mercedes had a rented car, most nights Mr. Gingrich drove her into Savannah. She seemed to like it. She told me that Mr. Gingrich was the first real friend she'd had. When I asked, "Don't you consider me a real friend?" she said, "The best. But George is the first friend I've had who happens to be a man."

And she was my best friend. Better than Sarah. I'd thought a lot about what Mercedes had told me. It was true what she said. She was still Mercedes.

"Wanda. Wanda," Momma called.

I knew what she was calling me for. Even though she was getting better about Poppa and his trying not to drink, once in a while she'd get crazy. "Take Poppa's lunch on down to the shop," she'd say, or "Poppa forgot to take his coffee money."

"Wanda."

"Coming."

And sure enough, she was at it again. "Wanda, would you take Poppa's lunch on down to the shop?" she said. "Can't have him going hungry."

I wanted to remind her about what Mercedes kept telling her. How nothing could stop Poppa from drinking but Poppa himself. Not talking to him about it, not telling him to go to more meetings, not checking up on him like she did. And not sending me to do it.

When I got to the shop, Mr. Gingrich was in the back. "How you doing?" he called out. "Come on back."

"Where's Poppa?" I said.

"Just called from Miz Love's. Said he was having trouble sorting things out. She claims the sink your poppa and I delivered isn't the one she ordered. That's not true. We got her signature on the dotted line stating she ordered model number two-eight-four-nine-Z . . ."

"Is he coming right back?"

"Can't be sure," he said. "He told me he had to stop off at MacPherson's —"

"Why?"

"Didn't say. Sometimes customers ask your poppa to meet them outside the shop here."

He stopped talking and looked at me for a long minute.

"Well," he said, "I best be leaving now. Miz Love's waiting on me."

"I'll wait awhile," I said.

"Okay," he said, "but if you leave before your poppa gets back, lock the front door and go out the back."

I waited for almost an hour; then I wrote Poppa a note telling him I'd put his lunch in the storeroom, where it was cool. Just as I was leaving, the telephone rang. It was Momma wanting to speak to Poppa. She wanted to know when he'd be back.

"Soon," I said.

"Where is he?"

"At Miz Love's."

"He said he was stopping by there on the way to the shop. He's still there?"

"I guess so."

"Soon as he comes in, you tell him to call," she said, her voice sounding upset.

"You all right?"

"I'm fine. It's Poppa I get worried for."

As soon as I hung up, I started to get that feeling in my stomach. I locked the front door and went out the back, but instead of starting for home, I walked in the direction of MacPherson's. I tried to shut Momma's voice out of my head, but I couldn't. My head kept telling me to go on home, but my feet kept walking toward MacPherson's. My heart pounded. My mouth was dry. Maybe things had been too good to last.

When I turned the corner, I saw Poppa standing just inside the entrance of MacPherson's. His back was to me and he was talking to somebody.

I stood still, barely breathing.

"Frank," I heard my father say, "you're making

things worse. Come on, now, I'll buy you a cup of coffee."

But the man turned away from him. "Go on home, Augie," the man said. "No use talking that kind of talk to me. It's not coffee I need."

My father put his arm around the man and the man began to cry.

I flattened my back against the wall, hoping Poppa wouldn't see me. It made me feel sick to my stomach, standing there like that. I dug my nails into my hands, and walked sideways until I got to the corner. I was getting like Momma, spying on Poppa like that. I felt ashamed.

I thought about Poppa being so gentle with his friend. Mercedes had told me how mean her stepfather was when he drank. "You're lucky having a poppa like him," she'd told me. "He's kind drunk or sober."

But I wanted him sober more than anything.

I took the long way back to the shop, and when I got there I heard my father talking to his friend in the back room, asking him if he wanted more coffee, asking him to help himself to more lunch.

"I owe you a lot," I heard his friend say.

"You'd do the same for me," my father said.

"I don't think I'm going to make it, Aug. I don't think I can." And then he cried.

I didn't want to hear any more. I tiptoed to the door and started for home.

Chapter 19

"Less than two weeks to go," Momma said, sewing up the sleeve of the dress she was making for April May. She'd been so busy sewing and cooking, she kind of forgot about everything else. More and more she wasn't saying "Wanda, put the clothes in the washing machine" or "Wanda, get fresh towels for the bathroom." She was changing more with Poppa. She'd ask him what he was doing down at the shop and how his meetings were going. She didn't go so far as to ask him to bring somebody home, but she did listen.

"I told Poppa to bring fresh bread when he comes home tonight," she said. "We're having a cold supper. I'll be too tired to cook."

"Momma, I won't be here," I said. "Don't you remember tonight's the night I go to Savannah with Mercedes?"

"Oh, that's right," she said, arching her back and

then rubbing it. "You have a good time." Then she held up the top of the dress and whispered, "Did you ever see anything so big?"

I laughed and so did she. "There's more yardage in this dress than in all the curtains in this house," she said. Then she looked down at her stomach. "I shouldn't poke fun," she said. "I'll be needing one bigger than this one very soon." And then she really laughed. It was good to hear. One night I'd heard her laugh at something Poppa said to her. "August," she'd said, "don't be fresh." And then she'd said, "Wanda might be awake." But she didn't stop. She giggled for a long time and it made me feel good all over.

"I'm going up to Mercedes to see what time we're leaving."

The thought of going to Savannah without Momma pleased me. And it pleased me even more that Momma hadn't made a fuss about it.

I knocked on Mercedes's door softly, hoping she was awake, but she didn't answer. I knocked again, but still she didn't answer. I walked back downstairs and when I got to the hall, I heard Mercedes talking on the telephone.

"George," she was saying, "I'm going to drive myself in early. I made an appointment to have my hair done this noon."

She ran her fingers through her hair and when she saw me, she waved.

"No," she said into the phone, "don't do that. I've

got something I have to do after the last show and I'll need my own car."

She rested her head on her elbow. "It came up at the last minute. I'm sorry." She listened for a minute, then sat upright and said, "Oh, I forgot about that. Oh, God, I hate to disappoint her, but I'll make it up to her tomorrow night." She nodded. "Okay, but it'll be late."

She stood up and stretched. "I'll talk to you tonight. Late. Okay?"

She hung up the phone and sighed. "Wanda," she said, "I'm sorry, sweetie, but I'm going to have to take you in tomorrow night instead of tonight. Is that okay with you?"

I was disappointed down to my shoes. But all I said to Mercedes was, "It's okay."

She kissed me quickly and said, "Something came up and I just can't cancel out."

I asked her what came up, but all she'd say was that she'd probably be late coming home. Then she asked me if I wanted to come on up to her room while she got ready.

I watched her dress, and when she finished tying back her hair and started toward the door, I told her I'd walk her to the car. "I want to check the mailbox," I said. "Maybe the letter came."

"What letter?"

"Elvis's," I said as we walked down the path toward her car.

"Sweetie, you just won't give up."

I ran over to the mailbox but it was empty. I felt as if maybe it would never come, but I didn't want Mercedes to know that. "If it comes when you're not here, can I open it?" I said as she started her car.

"Sure," she said, "why not." Then she blew me a kiss and was gone.

I could hear the whir of Momma's sewing machine floating up the stairs, and when I went by Mr. Collins's door he called out hello to me. He'd been quiet the last few days and I asked him if he was feeling all right.

"Just fine, Wanda. Just tending to my own business. Don't want to irk our friend in there," he said, motioning to April May's room. "I'm counting the days now."

"So is Poppa," I said and went down to my room. I put Elvis on the record player and stretched out on my bed to wait for the mailman. Maybe today it would come. I felt kind of like it would. I kept going back and forth to the window, and when I saw the mailman coming down the block, I raced downstairs. I got to the mailbox just as he was putting the mail in. I took it from him and ran to the glider to sort it out.

Mail for Mr. Collins as usual and bills for Poppa and a square card for April May and then, there it was: the letter. Elvis's letter. I looked at it for a long time: Mercedes Washington, R.D. 2 Marigold Place, Harmony, Georgia, and in the left-hand corner: Elvis Presley Live in Concert, c/o Dexter Auditorium, Savannah, Georgia.

My heart pounded in my chest.

I dropped the mail on the hall table, hugged the letter to me, and ran back to my room, where Elvis was still singing. I sat on the edge of my bed and looked at it again. I slipped my finger under the flap and eased it up. I didn't want to tear it or anything. It had to be perfect. I laid open the flap and reached inside and took it out. I opened it slowly and read it word by word:

Dear Mercedes:
Thank you for inquiring about the concert I'm to give at the Dexter Auditorium on September 5. It will be my pleasure to have you in the audience.

I stopped reading to catch my breath. "See," I said out loud, "I told you he'd remember you. And by your first name."

I read on. ". . . Savannah has always been one of my favorite cities and I look forward to being there with friends once again . . ."

— *Wait until Mercedes sees this. Just wait.*

". . . and you are among them . . ."

— *She's going to faint when she reads that.*

". . . Tickets are available directly at the box office . . ."

I held my breath.

— *I'll bet they're the best seats in the house.*

". . . or can be purchased by mailing the enclosed order form."

— *What's he talking about?*

". . . looking forward to seeing you in the audience, and again, thank you for your interest. Sincerely, Elvis Presley."

What did he mean by that? I wished Mercedes were here, she'd know. I didn't want to ask Momma, but I wanted to know, was he or wasn't he sending tickets? My stomach began to tighten. I shut the record player off and ran all the way to Poppa's shop.

When he started to read the letter he had a big smile on his face but as he read on, it left. He read it over again and then he folded it carefully, put his arm around me, and said, "Wanda, honey, this is a form letter. They send this out to everybody."

"You're wrong," I said. "He wouldn't do that."

"Honey, it's true." Poppa opened the letter again and pointed to the address and to the "Dear Mercedes." "See, hon?" he said. "This printing is different than the rest of the letter."

I looked closely and then gave the letter back to him. "That doesn't mean anything."

He sighed, looked at the letter again, and said softly, "She told you he wouldn't remember her."

"But she said she knew him. She said she wrote to him and he answered her."

"She did?"

"Yes."

"Maybe you misunderstood her."

I shook my head.

"Do you think maybe she made it all up?" I said, taking the letter from his hand.

"Do you think that?"

I looked at him for a long minute and then turned and ran out the door.

Chapter 20

A soft wind blew down the street; bits and pieces of paper rolled past my feet. My father called after me, but I didn't answer. I walked fast, wanting to be by myself.

— *Maybe Poppa's wrong. Maybe my letter went to one of Elvis's secretaries, somebody who doesn't know all of his friends. Maybe he never saw the letter, because even if he knew her for only two months, he'd remember her.*

I crossed over to Lotus Lane.

How could he forget somebody like Mercedes, even if her last name was different? I told him in the letter where they'd met.

— *Mercedes, please hurry home tonight. I need you to make this okay again.*

I opened the front door very quietly and tiptoed up the stairs. I didn't want to see anybody, but when I got to the top of the stairs, April May was standing in her doorway.

"Did I get any mail?"

"It's downstairs."

"Why didn't you bring it up?"

"I'll get it later."

"What's that you've got?"

"Nothing."

"The letter from what's his name?"

I ignored her.

"Telling you he doesn't remember Miss La-De-Da, I'll bet."

"It's none of your business."

"Don't you talk to me like that."

Mr. Collins called out to me not to pay any attention to her. "Be still, Wanda," he said. "Silence is strength."

"Oh, shut up, you old fool," April May said. "And as for you, I told you what she was. Her kind are full of untruths, but you didn't believe me, did you?"

"Watcha doin'? Watcha doin'? Watcha doin'?"

"Shut up. Both of you," I shouted and ran to my room. I stretched out on my bed and looked over at Elvis. He smiled at me from my dresser.

I looked at the letter again.

— *Poppa has to be wrong. Why would Elvis say he would be happy to have her in the audience? Why would he do that? And why would he say he looked forward to being with his friends and that Savannah was one of his favorite cities and that she was his friend? Why would he do that?*

Poppa *was* wrong. He had to be wrong.

I put the letter in my dresser drawer and picked up Elvis's picture. "Please," I whispered, "please remember her. It's awfully important to me and to her, too. April May will never shut up about this and that'll make Mercedes feel awfully bad."

"Wanda," my mother called, "I'll need you to help me for a few minutes."

"You shut up, too," I said under my breath.

"And another thing," I whispered to Elvis. "I've written to Sarah that I was going to meet you. Sarah's been so many places. She met Annette Funicello at Disneyland last year. I've never gone anywhere. I've never met anybody. Please."

"WANDA."

It was no use. I put Elvis on the bed and went down to the kitchen.

"I really need your help," my mother said, smiling up at me. "I need you to hold the end of the skirt up so I can finish the hem."

She handed me the skirt and I stood by the sewing machine as my mother's fingers guided the satiny material under the needle. Her foot pressed down on the pedal, making the machine go faster and faster.

"How much did this dress cost, Momma?"

"A lot."

"All of your saving-up money?"

"Not all."

"But a lot?"

She nodded her head.

"She's not worth it."

She stopped sewing and rested her hands in her lap.

She looked up at me and said, "Don't say that. Everybody is worth something."

I didn't say anything.

"She certainly isn't an angel, but she took care of your grandmother and Petey."

"You think keeping him in a cage the way she does is taking care of him?"

"Not really, but it's the only way she knows. He's the only thing that's really hers."

"Well, now she's got Mr. Murphy."

"Not yet," Momma said. "But she will." Then she looked up and said, "Please, Lord. We'd sure appreciate it." She looked so tired, and for the first time I noticed the lines around her eyes.

"I just want this whole affair to go smoothly for all of us."

"You're nice, Momma."

She took my hand and squeezed it. "So are you," she said, and started up the machine again.

When the last bit of hem had been sewn, we scooped the dress into our arms and brought it up to my parents' bedroom and laid it over the door of my mother's closet. "There aren't hangers big enough to hold this," she said. "I'm going to get April May to try it on tomorrow or the next day at the latest."

"Do you need me anymore?"

She shook her head. "You go on back and do what you were doing. I'm all set now." She looked up at me. "You all right? You look awfully tired."

"I'm fine, Momma."

"Well, I'm tired and my back hurts," she said. "You know, I never knew I was pregnant with you. No aches. Guess it's my age. Or maybe it's all this sewing." She smoothed the dress one last time. "Soon as Poppa comes home, we'll have supper. It's all fixed. You just bring April May her tray when it's time. That okay with you?"

"Sure, Momma."

When supper was over and the dishes were done and Poppa had gone off to a meeting, I went back up to my room. From my bedroom window, I could see Mr. Gingrich leaning against his car. He was smoking a cigar.

"Mr. Gingrich," I called out. "Did Mercedes tell you exactly when she'd be home?"

"Late. Hope she doesn't make it too late, 'cause tomorrow morning we kind of have plans to shop for a proper wedding gift for April May and her intended. You got any ideas?"

"No."

"Your momma might know. Mercedes thought a money gift might be in order, but that don't hold with me." He knocked his cigar against his shoe, pinched it between his fingers, and put it into his shirt pocket. "Maybe you can kind of feel April May out when you get a chance. Only got a few days before the big day."

Then he said good night and told me to have happy dreams.

But when I did dream, they weren't happy.

I dreamed I was in a room all by myself. I kept banging on the door, calling to somebody on the other side, but I couldn't get out. I banged and banged for a long time. It was so scary it woke me up. I got out of bed and just as I did, headlights came into the driveway. A man was standing in the light and when the car stopped, I realized it was Mr. Gingrich.

"Mercedes," I heard him say. "I've been waiting for you. I've got to talk to you."

"I'm exhausted," she said. "Can we make it quick?"

They went up to the porch and sat right below my room.

"I've got something to ask you," he said. "Something I've been wanting to ask you ever since that night we stopped off at the lake."

"You're starting up again, making more of that night than it was."

"More than it was? You call what we did nothing?"

"No, George. I was something that just happened."

"Not to me. It didn't just happen to me."

"And I never meant it to happen," she said.

"But it did."

"George, I told you that night that the most we could be was friends."

"I don't want to be friends. I'm forty-one years old, never married, never wanted to, and then you come into my life. I love you. Dammit to hell, Mercedes, I love you."

She didn't answer him. The night was cool and as still as a Sunday morning. I could hear the leaves rustling and the sound of the glider moving.

"Did you hear me?" he said, after a while.

"I told you not to do that," she said, her voice rising.

"What? Do what?"

"Love me."

"You think you can tell people not to love someone?"

She didn't answer him for a long time. Then she said, "I love you, too. The way friends love each other."

"That's nonsense talk."

"It's not nonsense. It's the truth."

"Don't you hear what I'm saying? I want to marry you."

There was another long silence and then she said, "From the beginning I told you it would never work out. Friendship is all I can give you."

"Folks sometimes start out as friends."

"That's all it can ever be with people like us, George."

"Don't you understand? I don't care. It don't matter to me."

"But it does to me," she said. "Besides, it's time I move on."

— *Move on. She's going to move on? She never told me that.*

Mr. Gingrich got up and stood at the railing.

"You got somebody else?"

"No."

"Then why do you have to go?"

Another long silence. "Because it's time. Way over time."

"Why'd you let me fall in love with you?" he said, his voice rising and cracking as if he were going to cry.

— Poor Mr. Gingrich. Why'd she do that? Fooling him, making him believe she loved him.

"We'd best take a walk or we're going to wake the whole house up," she said.

He went down the porch steps quickly, Mercedes running after him, and when she caught up to him she took his arm and they disappeared into the darkness.

— Does she do things like this all the time? Fool people. Like Mr. Gingrich? Me?

I took the letter from my dresser.

— Maybe she did make it up. "Why, Elvis and me were like this," she had told me. "I got my picture taken with Elvis."

"Maybe that's not her in the picture," I said out loud.

"That you, Wanda? Everything okay?"

"Yes, Poppa."

— And you, Poppa, you sided with her, telling me that maybe I misunderstood her.

I sat on the edge of my bed and waited, and when I heard Mr. Gingrich's voice and footsteps coming closer, I took the letter and tiptoed through my parents' bedroom. I stood in the dark, waiting until Mercedes went up to her room. Then I climbed the stairs to the attic.

I knocked on her door and when she asked who was there, I went in.

"What are you doing up at this hour?" she said, smiling at me. "You all right?"

"I'm fine," I said, handing her the letter.

The smile left her face. "What's wrong? There's something very wrong with you." She put her hand on mine.

I pulled my hand away.

"Please read it."

She read it quickly. Then she sat down in the rocking chair and read it again. She looked over at me and shook her head very slowly and said, "But I told you he wouldn't remember me."

"You told me you knew him. You told me you wrote to him. You showed me his picture. You told me he answered you."

"Wanda," Mercedes said, coming over to me, "I told you I knew him and that was the truth, and maybe I told you he wrote back to me because that's what you wanted to hear. But I didn't remember that he had. I may be a lot of things, but I'm not a liar."

"What do you call what you did to Mr. Gingrich?"

"What are you talking about?"

"You know what I'm talking about."

"No, sweetie, I don't."

"Don't call me that," I said, looking straight at her. "You know what you did. I heard you tonight. You made him think you loved him and that you were going to stay and marry him —"

"Oh, my God, Wanda, that's not true. That's simply not true. George knows that."

"That's not what he said. You lied to him. Just like you did to me. Telling me all that stuff, making me believe it was all true. And you even lied about what you really are."

"How can you say that after what I told you?" she said, reaching out to me.

I backed away from her. "You even fooled me into believing you were staying. You never told me you were leaving," I said.

She didn't answer me. She just stood there.

My head began to ache. "You shouldn't have done it," I said. "Making me think things were going to be so great. Making me believe I was going to be special. Even trying to make me believe that even if Poppa drinks again, things will still be okay. Well, they wouldn't be, and nothing is okay and it's your fault."

Mercedes shook her head. Her eyes were wide and her mouth was open, but still she said nothing.

"Well, you go on and leave. See if I care." My voice broke. "You can take this back, too," I said, pulling her ring from my finger. "I don't want to remember you."

Then I went over to the bed, pulled my quilt off, dropped the ring, and ran downstairs.

My mother was standing in the bedroom doorway.

"Wanda," she said. "What's going on? What are you dragging that around for?"

"Nothing, Momma. I got cold up there."

"What were you doing up there?"

"I had to talk to Mercedes."

"At this hour?"

"It was important. I couldn't wait."

"Is everything all right?"

"Fine."

"Then go back to sleep."

"In a minute," I said.

"You're sure you're all right?"

"I'm fine now. Good night, Momma."

She kissed the top of my head and said good night.

When I got into my room, I threw the quilt in the corner. Then I picked up the arm of my record player and dug the needle back and forth into Elvis. "I don't need you either," I whispered. I took his picture from the dresser and threw it under my bed. Then I sat by my window until my eyes wouldn't stay open anymore and it was time for sleep.

Chapter 21

"You look lovely, April May," my mother said, taking the last fat roller from April May's head. "Doesn't she, August?"

"Just like that little bride doll my mother used to put on her bed," Poppa said, winking at my mother. "Remember that doll, April May?"

"I surely do," she said, smiling at him and telling him how sweet he was, how good Momma was to have sewn her wedding dress for her, and how nice I'd been to help her pack her clothes for her move over to Mr. Murphy's house. She even said something about how good Mercedes had been to loan her a rhinestone crown for her head and to agree to sing at the wedding. But I knew better. April May hadn't even wanted her to be at the wedding. But Poppa told her that Mercedes was coming and she'd be doing the singing or there'd be no singing. "Well," I heard April May tell Mr. Murphy, "it'll mean one more gift."

"We were happy to do it, April May," my mother said. "Weren't we, August?"

"Yes, ma'am," he said. "We certainly were mighty glad to do anything we could to make this day a memorable one."

My mother, standing behind April May, rolled her eyes and whispered, "Amen to that."

"You all have been so nice to me since Henry proposed. I feel happy that I'm marrying Murph, but I got me this funny feeling. Like a child going to kindygarten for the first time." Then she got this dreamy look on her face and said, "April May Murphy. *Mrs.* April May Murphy." She sighed and said, "I surely have got to get used to that."

"So do we, April May," my mother said. "It'll take time."

My father put his arm around me and headed me toward the door. "It'll take me all of three seconds to get used to it," he whispered. "How about you?"

"Two," I whispered back.

"And Momma?"

"One."

He shut the door behind us and said, "Calvin told me this morning that this is one time when absence will not make the heart grow fonder." He slipped his arm into mine and led me toward the porch. "Come on," he said, "let's watch out for the Murphys. Got to make sure they get into the right house."

I sat on the glider and my father perched himself on the porch railing. I raised my dress up a little and looked at my legs. This was the first time I'd ever worn nylon stockings. Momma had bought them for me. And she'd bought me new shoes. They were blue. The same blue of the dress Mercedes had given me the day she came. That day seemed so long ago.

I'd wanted a new dress but my mother wouldn't hear of it. "You are wearing that dress, Wanda," my mother had said. "Just because you are angry at Mercedes does not mean that we are going out and spending money on another dress. Besides," she'd added, "it's high time you made amends to Mercedes. Whether you're ready to admit it or not, she wasn't the one at fault."

"You look awfully pretty, Wanda," my father said. "I'll be so proud to introduce you and Momma to Frank."

Poppa had told Momma he invited his friend Frank to the wedding. Momma started to say something about did he think it was a good idea, but Poppa just said, "I want him here."

I went over to the porch railing and leaned against it. I could smell the honeysuckle. "Can I ask you something, Wanda?"

"Sure, Poppa."

"Don't you think you should speak to Mercedes and maybe say you're sorry?"

"Why? I didn't tell her things that weren't true."

"Neither did she."

"Why do you and Momma keep saying that?"

My father swung his legs back and forth. "You know, Wanda, sometimes we want something so bad, we start off thinking it's true, but really knowing it's not. Then somewhere along the line, a little part of us believes it's true. Then a little bit more of us believes it. Until finally all of us believes it. You know what I'm saying?"

"She shouldn't have told me all those things. Fooling me like that."

"Did she?" he said.

"Yes. She fooled all of us, not telling us what she really is. And she fooled Mr. Gingrich."

"Wanda, what's that got to do with anything?"

"Mr. Gingrich wants to marry her."

"I don't mean George. I mean her fooling us. Why are you judging her like that?"

I turned away.

"Folks are folks, Wanda. No one's got a right to judge what people do to get along in this life. Look at me. You know how hard it's been these last few weeks."

"I know, Poppa."

"Do you? I don't know if anybody does."

He hopped off the railing and came over to me. "You know, I used to pretend that I could stop drinking anytime I wanted to. But it wasn't true, Wanda. It took a lot more than pretending for me to stop."

"What's that got to do with Mercedes telling me all that stuff?"

"What I'm saying is that most people pretend sometimes. You. Me. A lot of people. But some of us pretend so long that it almost seems real."

He looked out beyond the honeysuckle. "The night you and Momma went into Savannah was the night I stopped pretending. When I woke up and found your mother gone and you with her, I thought that was it. I don't ever remember being so scared, thinking I'd lost you both."

"It wasn't Momma's idea to go. I kind of tricked her into going."

"That was no trick. It was a miracle, because it was that night I decided I'd had my last drink." He took a deep breath. "It wasn't easy. It's not easy now, but that's what I'm doing."

"I love you, Poppa," I said.

"I love you, too. And I love your momma. And I'm going to love this new baby. And you know what, Wanda?" he said, looking straight at me. "I'm getting to love me. It's been a long time coming, this feeling good about myself. And knowing I can do it."

I hugged him hard.

"It'd be good for you to go on up to Mercedes."

I shook my head. "Why should I be the one? I didn't do anything to her."

But that wasn't entirely true.

"Because she's your friend," he said.

I turned away from him. "Not anymore."

He didn't say anything.

"Besides, she probably won't want to talk to me. I said mean things."

"Between friends, mean things are forgiven. That's true. Else Momma and I would have been a memory long gone."

I didn't say anything.

"You think about it."

He kissed me quickly and said, "Wanda, my love, I think that's Mr. Murphy's car coming on up the block. Yes, Miss Dohr, I do believe I see my dear sister's groom making his way up Marigold Place." He looked up, clasped his hands together, and said, "Thank you, Lord, for this day, and thank you, Lord, for giving Mr. Murphy the courage to go through with this. For that we are truly thankful. Only You know how thankful we are for that."

I walked into the house, my mind still racing. I started up the stairs to the attic, but when I got to the landing, I couldn't seem to make my way up to the top. I walked back down the stairs very slowly. Momma was in the dining room, fixing the table. She put the punch bowl in the center. "Taste it for me, will you, Wanda?" she said, passing me a cup. "See if it's bubbly enough."

"It's fine, Momma," I said, putting the cup back on the table. "It really is."

"Well, I don't know if everybody else will think it's fine. Mr. Murphy's mother wanted something stronger," she said, rubbing her back with both hands, "as did Mr. Murphy himself. Did I tell you that?"

"Yes, Momma."

There was a lot of commotion in the hall and I heard my father say, "Well, well, now, Henry, you look mighty handsome. And just wait till you see April May."

Then he poked his head into the dining room. "They're all here," he said, smiling. "Jane Ann, Reverend Packs is setting himself up in the living room and

Mercedes is waiting at the piano for you." Then he turned to me and said, "You ready, Wanda?"

"Yes, Poppa."

"The bouquets are in the refrigerator," my mother said. "Make sure you get the right one. April May's is bigger."

"Come on," my father said, "let's go get the bride. Don't want to give anybody time to think. Especially Mr. Murphy."

Chapter 22

When we heard the "Wedding March," my father took April May's arm and started toward the top of the stairs.

"Go on, Wanda," he said. "You go ahead of us."

I went down the stairs slowly, as my mother had told me to, and walked into the living room. Mr. Murphy was standing by Mr. Packs, wearing a dark blue suit and a polka-dot tie. His hair was all slicked down. He was smiling, his wax teeth all yellow-looking. His best man, his brother Calhoun, was next to him, grinning. He had no teeth. Mercedes was at the piano, sun shining on her hair.

— Maybe Poppa was right. Maybe I did fool myself.

"Who gives this woman to be married to this man?"

"I do," my father said. "I certainly do."

— Momma told me Mercedes thought it would be a good idea if she moved into April May's room when April May left. "That way, Wanda gets her room back," she told my mother.

After today, April May will be gone forever. I should have gone up to Mercedes. Should have said I was sorry.

"And by the power given to me by the state of Georgia, I now pronounce you man and wife."

April May gazed up at Mr. Murphy. The crown Mercedes had lent her had tilted a little, making April May look like she was going to fall. But Mr. Murphy smiled down at her as though he had never seen anything as beautiful.

"You may kiss the bride," Mr. Packs said.

I didn't want to see that. I looked over at my mother. She was smiling. So was my father. Mercedes, too. She had a funny expression on her face, almost as if she were going to cry.

"And now, before they commence to greet their guests and the party gets under way," Mr. Packs said, "let's offer up a prayer of thanksgiving for this day." He asked everybody to join hands.

Mr. Murphy's mother was crying and she kept saying, "I'm losing my baby. I'm losing my baby." Mr. Packs told her to stop her crying and to get on with things. "Besides," he said, "Henry's almost past middle age. Time he took himself a wife." Mr. Murphy's sister, Odell, said a loud "Harumph." Then she took her mother's hand, motioned for her daughter, Lacey Jean, to take her grandmother's other hand, and said, "Let's get this over with."

Mr. Packs adjusted his glasses, bowed his head, and said, "Dear Lord, bless Henry and April May as they begin their walk down the path of life together. And may April May look as beautiful to Henry on their fiftieth wedding anniversary as she does this day. Amen."

— In fifty years, I'll be almost sixty-four. Momma and Poppa will be very old. Even the baby will be old.

"Amen," my father said. "AAMEN."

Then my mother played the piano and Mercedes sang "Oh Promise Me." Mr. Murphy and April May walked through the parlor, me behind them, and onto the porch. Bo Turner, Mr. Murphy's nephew, ran ahead of me and tripped on April May's dress, but April May didn't seem to notice. She greeted all the guests and Mr. Murphy introduced everybody to his mother and brother and his whole family. After everybody knew everybody else, my mother asked everyone to gather under the elm tree for picture taking. "Mercedes and George gifted April May with the camera, and George has graciously offered to act as photographer," she said. "After that, refreshments. Lord knows, there's plenty."

"You look like a little doll," I heard Mr. Murphy say to April May as I took my place under the tree.

"And you look like Cary Grant," she said.

I almost got sick to my stomach.

I watched Mr. Gingrich posing April May and Mr. Murphy. Mercedes stood back, watching. It made me think of the night I heard Mercedes and Mr. Gingrich outside my bedroom window.

Mr. Gingrich made April May and Mr. Murphy pose looking at one another, and holding hands with one another, and kissing one another. After about the fiftieth picture, Mr. Gingrich said, "Augie, come on. You, too, Miz Dohr, get in the picture. After all, Augie, you gave April May away and Miz Dohr, why, you've been laboring for days to give this fine party."

"Aaah," Mr. Collins said from the porch, "labor is the blessing of the earth."

My mother took my father's arm and stood beside April May and smiled a big wide smile. My father smiled wider. They looked almost like they did in their wedding picture — my father's arm around my mother's waist, her looking up at him, her eyes just for him. And when Mr. Gingrich took the last picture, my father took her in his arms and kissed her the way I'd never seen him kiss her before. I thought she'd get all embarrassed, seeing as everybody was watching, especially my father's friend, who she never even met before. But she didn't. She didn't tell him to stop, and when he let her go she just smoothed his hair, kissed his cheek quickly, and then the two of them walked back into the house.

"Now, April May," Mr. Gingrich said, "how about a portrait of the bride alone?"

She shook her head, but Mr. Murphy said, "That's fine with me, sugar babe, 'cause I want a picture with just my little doll in it." Then he disappeared into the house. So did Calhoun.

When the last picture was taken, and the music started, April May gathered up her dress and started back to the house. "Let's eat," she said. "Murph?" she called out as she struggled up the porch stairs, her dress catching on her high heels. "Where are you?"

"In the dining room, sweet one. Cal's getting ready to toast us."

"Well, tell him to make it short. I'm starved."

We all gathered around the dining room table as my father ladled out the punch. He looked so happy, his eyes shone. My mother stood beside him, her head to one side, a tiny smile on her face. "Wanda, honey," my father said, "would you help me pass out the punch glasses?"

"Sure," I said.

"Make sure Lacey Jean's cup ain't too filled," Odell said. "Bo's, too. Don't want them blamed for messing up the rug."

I nodded my head and passed the glasses, and when everyone held a glass, Calhoun raised his high and said, "To my big brother, Henry, and his sweet little wife." Then he slurped down the punch in one gulp. So did Mr. Murphy.

"I'm too hungry for punch," April May said, putting two chicken legs on her plate. She munched on one and held the other for Mr. Murphy. "Can't eat that," he said, downing another glass of punch. "Not till I get me some store teeth."

"I'd like to make a toast," Mr. Collins said. But before he could, April May and Mr. Murphy walked out of the room. "Old bag of wind," I heard April May say as she passed me.

One of Mr. Murphy's friends played the fiddle and

everybody yelled for Mr. Murphy to dance with April May, but she was too busy eating.

I helped myself to some chicken and headed toward the porch. It was crowded. The whole Murphy family, except for Mr. Murphy, was stretched out all over the front end, taking every single chair. Lacey Jean was dancing and running around yelling for wedding cake and Mrs. Murphy was still crying. Odell was telling her to hush up, that worse things happen.

"Now stop your fussing and take off your hat," she said. "The feather's gone soft and it's hanging in your plate."

I walked to the back of the porch. Mercedes was sitting on the steps with Mr. Gingrich, nodding and laughing at something he was saying. I leaned against the house and watched them. The fiddle played and the music drifted all around. I watched for a long, long time. Mercedes did most of the talking and Mr. Gingrich laughed a lot. It reminded me of all the times I went up to Mercedes's room and we sat and talked. And laughed. I missed those times. I missed her. I closed my eyes and thought about that first trip to Savannah. How good it was to be there, listening to her sing. How good it was to see Momma having such a good time. And Poppa starting not to drink. I thought about the day she'd told me about her real father and how she felt about what April May had called her.

"Hey, there, Wanda," somebody said. "Are you holding up the house?"

I opened my eyes and Mr. Gingrich was standing

there. "What are you doing here all by yourself? Why, the party's in full swing and you haven't eaten a thing." He picked up my plate and glass from the porch floor and said, "Come on, now. You're going to sit with Mercedes and me. Can't be celebrating by yourself."

I shook my head.

"We won't take no for an answer," he said. "Will we, Mercedes?"

"No," she said.

"Can I get you more punch?" he asked Mercedes.

Mercedes nodded.

"I'll tell you something," Mr. Gingrich said, holding up his punch glass, "if I didn't know your momma better, I'd swear I was getting a little drunk on this."

"It's the heat, George," Mercedes said.

I sat down on the step below her and spread my napkin on my lap and started to eat some chicken.

"Good chicken," she said. "Your momma really outdid herself."

I nodded.

"You look real pretty, Wanda," she said. "That dress does more for you than it ever did for me."

I put the chicken down and started to get up.

"Don't," she said.

"I have to," I said. "I just remembered Momma asked me to take the cake out of the refrigerator so it'll be easier to slice."

"Really?" she said.

She put her hand out. "Wanda, stay awhile," she said. "I'll help you later."

I could feel my eyes filling up. I stood up quickly, knocking the punch glass over, the red liquid spilling down the stairs. I picked up my plate and said, "Excuse me. I'm sorry, but I have to do it now."

"We should talk," she said, gathering her dress into her lap, away from the punch that was inching its way to where she sat.

"I've got to get the cake," I said and ran toward the kitchen.

"I'll help you," she called.

But I shook my head. "I can do it," I called back. "Thanks anyway."

I closed the kitchen door behind me and leaned against it, glad to be by myself, sorry that I hadn't told her I was sorry. Poppa had been right. I should have listened to him instead of holding on to all of it.

"August," I could hear my mother call. "August, is that you?"

The kitchen door opened. "Oh, it's you, Wanda. You seen Poppa?"

I shook my head.

"That's funny. He was here just a while ago. Better take the cake out now."

"That's what I'm doing."

"Good," she said. "I hope Poppa gets back soon. We're out of ice."

The cake was beautiful. It had taken my mother two days to bake and frost it. She'd tinted the frosting pink and across the top of the cake she'd written in white lettering "April May and Henry Murphy — August 22,

1964, to Forever." My father had added "Please, God," but my mother made him take it off.

I got the cake server from the kitchen drawer and started into the dining room. Momma was clearing off the table, making room for the cake. "My back is stiff, my feet hurt, and I'm hot," she said, raising her shoulders and arching her back. "I'll be happy to put my feet up and rest tonight."

"You're doing too much, Momma. Go sit down."

She shook her head. "I'm kind of enjoying it, and you and Poppa have been a real big help."

She swept the last of the crumbs from the table and said, "I think I'm going to have some punch. Maybe it'll cool me off."

She put the glass to her lips and took a sip. And then another. And another. Then she dipped the ladle into the punch bowl and put it to her lips. "Oh, dear God."

"What is it, Momma?"

"Nothing, Wanda. You put the cake on back in the fridge."

"But Momma . . ."

"Go on, now. Do as I say. We'll wait for Poppa before we cut the cake."

She smoothed her hair and walked out of the house and onto the porch. "Mr. Murphy," she called. "I've got to speak to you."

Chapter 23

"What something? And when did you put it in?" I heard my mother say.

"Vodka," Mr. Murphy said. "Calhoun put vodka into the batch of punch you had sitting out in the kitchen. That's all, just some vodka."

"That's all?" she said.

"Just enough to give it a kick, Miz Dohr. Calhoun didn't mean no harm. Sure didn't mean to . . ."

"Where's August?"

"He asked to borry my car a while back. He said his friend needed a ride, and I didn't mind so I . . ."

"Oh, God," Momma said. "Oh, my God."

I stood still, my face hot, my stomach sick. "Oh, Poppa," I whispered. "Poppa."

"You had no right," I could hear my mother say. "You are guests in my home."

"What's happening out here?" April May said, grabbing my arm. "What's going on?"

"Calhoun put vodka in the punch," I said. My tongue felt heavy in my mouth. "Poppa had some."

"All this fuss for that? It's not like he never had a drink before."

She didn't understand. She didn't understand anything. Nobody did.

"I'm real sorry, ma'am," Mr. Murphy said, trailing after my mother. "We didn't mean no harm."

"Just leave," my mother said, walking back into the house. "Please," she said. "Just leave. All of you."

April May started to mumble something about how ridiculous my mother was acting. Her fat arms puffed out below the sleeves of her wedding dress. The dress my mother had made for her. The dress my mother had spent her saving-up money on. And here she was smiling and prancing around the room as if she were a princess or something instead of a fat old lady.

"I sure hope this don't cause hard feelings," Mr. Murphy said.

"I'm going on up to change," April May said. "It's no wonder poor Aug drinks, him having to put up with all this."

I wanted to hit her. I wanted to hit her so bad I had to clench my fists.

She looked over at me and said, "And I'm not leaving Petey. I'm taking him with me now."

"You do that, sweet bun," Mr. Murphy said. Then, turning to my mother, he said, "Sure didn't mean to cause no trouble."

"We'll go home in Calhoun's car," Odell said. "Kids are getting restless and April May's probably going to take her sweet time."

Then she called for Calhoun, told Lacey Jean to stop whining about not getting any cake, yanked Bo from the glider by the hair, took her mother by the arm, and they were gone.

My mother stood in the hall, her back against the wall, her hair brushing against her wedding picture, her face pale.

"Momma," I said, "you're getting yourself all upset and you don't know that Poppa's gone drinking or anything."

She said nothing.

"You'll see. He's all right."

"Oh, God, I hope so," she said. "But it's happened before, and once he starts, it seems like he can't stop himself."

"This time is different, Momma. Poppa told me."

She sighed and held out her hand. I took it and we walked slowly out to the kitchen. She sat at the table and rubbed the tablecloth. Around and around her hand went. I could hear Mercedes saying good-bye to people, telling them that it would be best not to disturb my mother.

"I'll make you tea," I said.

She shook her head. "I'll do it. I want to move around. My whole body is stiff. I've been feeling like this all day."

Momma pushed herself away from the table and went to the stove. The sun, low in the sky, lit up the kitchen floor.

She picked up the kettle but it dropped from her hand. "Wanda," she called, bending over the stove. "Help me."

"What is it, Momma?" I ran over to where she stood and when I did, she looked at me and said, "Oh, God, no. Tell me it's not happening."

She grabbed my arms, squeezed them quickly and then just as quickly let them go.

"Momma, what is it? Tell me. What's the matter?"

"Something's happening. I'm losing —" Her face was as white as the stove.

"Poppa's not gone. You'll see. He'll be back."

"The baby. The baby," she said. Her whole body slumped. "Get Mercedes."

But before I could, Mercedes was beside us calling out to Mr. Gingrich to get an ambulance.

We helped my mother ease her way onto the floor. I wanted to run and hide, but I took her head in my lap and held her. I stroked her hair and wiped the sweat from her forehead with my dress. She shivered and Mercedes tucked a tablecloth around her.

"August," Momma called softly.

"He's coming, Momma. I know it." I rocked her head back and forth. Little bits of blood seeped into the tablecloth, and it was Momma's favorite. My back heaved up and down, but no sound came.

"Wanda."

"Yes, Momma. I'm here."

She looked up at me, tears spilling from her eyes. "Just when everything was going to be all right," she said. Her voice was a soft, distant drum.

"It will be all right. I love you, Momma."

She tried to reach up, but she couldn't.

"Murph," I heard April May call from the hall. "I'm all set to go." And from the porch, I heard Mr. Gingrich shout, "In here. She's in here." And then two men raced into the kitchen carrying a stretcher. They took my mother's head from my lap and picked her up gently. Her arms stretched out and her legs hung down like a doll's. They put her on the stretcher and covered her with a blanket.

I kissed her good-bye and told her I loved her again. But she didn't answer me.

April May stood in the doorway, shopping bags at her feet, Petey in his cage.

"What's going on?" April May said.

"Watcha doin'? Watcha doin'?"

"Excuse us, lady," one of the men said. "Coming through."

Mr. Murphy picked up her bags and when my mother passed him, he said, "I'm sure sorry, ma'am. Sorry as I can be."

I ran down the hall and onto the porch. I stood at the railing, taking deep breaths, watching the men carry my mother toward the ambulance. It was so ugly. The paint was dirty and the glass around the flashing light was broken. The men put Momma inside and just as they did, Mr. Murphy's car pulled up to the curb. My father leapt out and ran over to the ambulance, shouting, "What's happened? What's wrong?" I tried to call out to him, but he didn't hear me. One of the men helped him climb into the back of the ambulance. Then the doors closed and the sound of the siren filled the air. I ran after the ambulance as it went down the driveway, and when it got to the curb, the wheels bounced hard.

"Be careful," I shouted. "You be careful. Momma's inside." Then I walked back to the porch slowly. So slowly it seemed a million miles away.

"Watcha doin'? Watcha doin'?" Petey called.

He was sitting on the swing in his cage. "Poor Petey," I said. The sound of the siren got softer and softer and when it disappeared into the air, I picked up Petey's cage. "You want to get out?" I said.

"Hello. Hello."

I opened the door to the cage and whispered, "Well, come on. It's okay."

He waited for a while, not sure of what to do; then he flapped his wings and flew out. He flew around the porch and then perched on the rosebush.

"Go on," I said. "Nothing's holding you now."

"What do you think you're doing?" April May called out of a window. "You put Petey back in there."

"Go on," I said. "Go."

April May stormed out of the house. "You get in your cage," she screamed at Petey. "NOW."

But Petey didn't. He flapped his wings and flew from the rosebush, to the honeysuckle vine, and up to the willow tree, his wings beating the air, parting the leaves of the willow.

"Get back here," April May shouted.

But Petey didn't. His wings kept beating.

"Good-bye, Petey," I shouted. "Go."

He dipped down once, then flew down the path and out over the street.

"Stop! Stop!" April May shouted.

But Petey kept flying. I could see his wings outlined against the sky. I stood watching until I couldn't see him anymore, wanting to believe that he was calling back a good-bye to me.

"Look what you've done," April May screamed. "You wicked thing."

And then Mercedes was beside me. She put her arm around me and led me to the door.

"God will punish you for this," April May screamed. "And you," she said, pulling at Mercedes's arm. "You think you're getting away with what you've done. Soon as I get out of here, I'm telling everybody just what you are."

"Be quiet, April May," Mercedes said, taking the cage from my hand. She smoothed my hair and walked me back into the house and up to the bathroom. She ran water into the sink. She led me to the tub and made me sit down. She wiped my face with cool water. She washed my hands. And when she was finished, she sat beside me. We sat for a long, long time, not speaking.

A warm breeze blew against the screen and into the room and onto my face. The sun crept slowly across the window, and when the last bit of sunshine disappeared, I called out for my mother. I closed my eyes and looked up and asked God not to let her die and to let us have the baby. And then I turned to Mercedes and held on to her until I couldn't cry anymore.

Chapter 24

It seemed like forever before Poppa called from the hospital and told me that Momma was going to be all right. "Momma wants to see you, honey."

"You sure she's all right?"

"I'm sure."

"And the baby? What about the baby?"

"I don't know." His voice broke. "He's so tiny."

A knot came in my stomach. Up to now, it was just a baby I didn't even care about, but now it was different.

Poppa told me to pray and then he asked to speak to Mr. Gingrich.

"Sure thing, Augie. No problem. Be glad to do it. And I'm sure sorry things worked out the way they did."

"Please, God," I whispered, "take care of him."

"Wanda," Mr. Gingrich said, "your poppa asked me to drive you on down to the hospital."

Mercedes stood at the door. "Why don't you change, sweetie. I'll go with you."

I looked down at my dress. It was streaked and dirty. "I wanted to clean up for Momma. She doesn't like the house to be a mess," I said, not really wanting to go to the hospital, afraid to go, knowing if I saw the baby, he'd be real and then if he died —

"We'll do it later, won't we, George?"

"Sure thing. You go on now and change."

When I went into my room, it was so still I could hear my father's clock ticking in my parents' room. It made me think of the day Momma felt the baby move. "Wanda," she'd called from her bedroom. "Come quick."

And when I got there, she'd lifted her blouse and put my hand on her stomach. The room was still then, too. And the clock ticked.

"Momma," I'd said. "you sure?"

She'd nodded and pressed my hand harder. I'd held my breath and waited. And then I'd felt something. Just below my mother's breast I'd felt something moving. "Yes," I'd said, "I feel it." Something had pushed at my hand. It was something I'd never felt before. Like a small wave, only silent and warm. But it wasn't real. Even when I'd put my cheek on her stomach and felt it again, it wasn't really real.

"Wanda," Mercedes called. "It's time to go."

I folded my dress and placed it on my bed, smoothing the skirt. "I'm ready," I called.

The hospital was as ugly as the ambulance. The corridors smelled of iodine. My father was waiting at the information desk and when he saw me he walked over. He hugged me for a long minute; then we walked down the hall and onto the elevator. When it stopped, he led me to my mother.

She was lying in bed, her face flushed, her hair spread out on the pillow. When she saw me, she held her arms out and I ran to her, putting my head next to hers. She held me and whispered what I didn't want to hear.

"The baby, Wanda. He came early. And he's so little. Too little."

My father stood at the window, looking out. "He may not make it," he said.

"It's nobody's fault," Momma said. "He just came too soon. These things happen, the doctor said. Do you hear me, Wanda?"

"I hear you, Momma."

I could feel her breath on my cheek, moist and warm. She smoothed my hair, and after a while her hand slipped from my head and she slept.

My father stared out the window, not speaking. I went over to him and put my hand in his.

"I didn't drink," my father said after a long while.

"That's good," I whispered, squeezing his hand, my breath coming easier.

"Frank did, so I thought it'd be best to get him out of there. I didn't think your mother would miss me. I thought I'd be back in a few minutes, but he gave me a hard time."

"You did what you had to do."

He squeezed my hand. "And left all the mess to you."

"It's all right, Poppa. You heard Momma. It was nobody's fault."

A nurse came into the room and told us it would be best to let my mother sleep. I kissed her cheek and my father told me he'd take me down to where Mr. Gingrich and Mercedes were waiting. When we were almost there, I turned to my father and said, "I want to see him."

My hands were cold and that old feeling was back in my stomach as we headed toward the nursery.

When we got there a nurse wheeled him over to the window. He was the tiniest thing I ever saw. He was dark red and had a lot of black hair.

I looked at him for a long time, thinking about how I hadn't even wanted him. Now I was whispering to him, telling him I loved him and how much we all needed him. Asking him not to leave us.

After a while, my father took my arm. "Time to go. They'll be wondering what happened."

When we got home Mercedes helped me clean up the kitchen. I put Momma's good things away and by the time we were through, there was nothing left of the party. Not even the cake. April May must have taken it.

* * *

After everything was done, the house was quiet.

Mercedes had her late show to do and Mr. Gingrich drove her into Savannah. She hadn't wanted to go, but when I told her I needed to be alone, she understood.

"Mr. Collins is right up in his room," she'd said. "And your poppa's only a phone call away."

When they were gone, I walked through the house. It was so quiet, so empty, except for Mr. Collins. I went up to my room and got the bear from my bed. Then I went from room to room, touching the tops of tables, smoothing the curtains, fingering the piano. I took the wedding picture from the wall and tried to find where Momma and Poppa had been cut apart. I thought about how I'd imagined it to be an omen. I looked at the picture for a long time. Momma was in the hospital, Poppa with her, the baby, too, but they were here, with me, filling up the space around me.

I walked out to the porch. Petey's cage was standing in the corner, empty. I stretched out on the glider. There was a new moon in the sky, the one Poppa was always looking for, saying it was good luck to see one. I thought about all the things that had happened this summer. Mercedes coming and Momma and I going to Savannah and Poppa not drinking. And Elvis. And Poppa's trip to New York. The wedding. Petey. And the baby.

A car's headlights lit up the porch. I heard an unfamiliar voice and then I heard my father's voice call out, "I thank you kindly. I appreciate it more than I can say."

I got up from the glider, the bear in my arms, and

watched my father walk up the driveway, the car's lights silhouetting him against the dark night. When he climbed the stairs and reached the porch, the light from the hall lit up his face. And even though Poppa was crying and didn't speak a word, I knew the baby was going to come home.

Chapter 25

The baby *is* going to make it. He's almost five weeks old now. He's still the littlest thing I ever saw. But now he's bald and pink. Momma came home. She hated to leave the baby in the hospital but the doctor said he'd have to stay for a while. She goes down to the hospital every day to feed him. I love to go with her. Poppa does, too. We stand and wave and talk to him and tell him he's coming home soon. I tell him he's going to be sleeping in the sun porch right near Momma and Poppa. And that that's where he should be. For now. But then I tell him that when he needs a room of his own, he'll have it.

So many other things are happening, too. Mr. Gingrich is moving into his own apartment on Lotus Lane. He told Mercedes he'd wait for her forever. And Mercedes moved into April May's room so I could have my room back. It won't be for long, though. Mercedes staying, I mean. She got another gig in New York.

Momma told me I could get new curtains and paint my furniture. But I didn't want to. I wanted everything to stay the same, just the way it always was.

Sometimes when I'm sitting there all by myself, I think I wouldn't mind being down in April May's old room. I think how good it would be to always have Mercedes up in mine, sitting in the rocking chair, waiting for me.

April May finally moved to Claxton with Henry and his mother and Calhoun. Poppa made me telephone and apologize to her for letting Petey out. I wasn't sorry and neither was Poppa, but he said we owed her that. I even told her I'd get her another bird. "Don't do me no favors," she said. "I've got enough to do taking care of this crew."

And I got to see Elvis. Sarah and I went. Mercedes bought the tickets and I thought she was going to go with us, but when the time came she said she had her own show to do.

I didn't want to go without her, but she told me if I didn't, she'd feel bad. "Please," she'd said, "you go and have yourself a good time." Then she laughed and said, "Besides, I'd rather see Little Richard."

Mercedes drove us into Savannah and treated Sarah and me to supper at her club. Then she called a taxi to take us to Dexter Auditorium. There were about a million people there. People selling shirts and records and pieces of what was supposed to be Elvis's hair. I wanted to buy some for Mercedes, but I couldn't get through the crowd. Sarah and I climbed so many stairs to get to our seats, we puffed for about an hour trying to catch our breath. There was smoke everywhere. It curled around the lights and made everything soft-looking, like fog does. People were screaming for Elvis to come out onstage.

He came out after a long, long time. And he *was* fixing his hair. "What'd I tell you?" I could hear Mercedes say even though she wasn't beside me.

And he sparkled. He wore a white satin suit with shiny beads all over it that glistened in the spotlight. His boots were white and had tassels that jumped around when he walked. He really sparkled. So did his guitar.

I sat there and watched him. He patted the top of his hair and then smoothed the sides and the back. The music started. It was so loud I could feel it beating inside me. And then he started to sing. Everybody was quiet when he sang but when he stopped, they screamed and stamped their feet.

"Elvis. Elvis. Shake that pelvis," somebody yelled from behind us. "Give us your blue suede shoes, Elvis, honey," another somebody yelled. It was worse than when people yelled at Mercedes during her show.

"Isn't he great?" Sarah said.

"He's beautiful," I said. But I don't think Sarah heard me because the whole audience stood up and pounded their feet on the floor and shouted at him. He sang again, moving around the stage. His guitar moved up and down with his body and his legs vibrated. The more he moved, the noisier the audience got. I couldn't hear him, but my eyes never left him. Then somebody came out onstage and told the audience if they didn't settle down, Elvis would stop singing. Everybody quieted down for a long time, but when Elvis said his last song would be "Can't Stop Loving You," everyone went crazy again. He waited until things settled down. I sat at the edge of my seat. The lights dimmed. My eyes burned and blurred.

"Thank you, you've been a good audience," Elvis said. And then he sang. *"Well, I can't stop loving you, 'cause I've made up my mind . . ."* He flew around the stage and people began to clap in time to the music and then the whole audience sang along with him. ". . . *And I can't stop wanting you . . .*"

He sang it three times and when he finished, he bowed and smiled and waved. We clapped and cheered and stamped our feet. And then he was gone, but we kept clapping and cheering and stamping, hoping he'd come back. But he didn't, and after a long while we followed the crowd down the stairs, out of the auditorium, and waited for Mercedes to pick us up. And when she did, Sarah got into the backseat. I sat up front with Mercedes.

"How'd you like him?" Mercedes asked.

Sarah told her how great he was and how noisy it all had been. I didn't say anything.

We drove out of Savannah, leaving the lighted buildings behind. Their windows looked as though there were millions of fireflies flying around inside. I thought about the very first night I'd come to Savannah, to hear

Mercedes sing, the night I saw the Elvis sign and all that had happened since that night.

"Did you enjoy it, sweetie?" Mercedes said after a while.

"Yes."

"Was he all you expected?"

I nodded my head.

He was beautiful and I still loved him. I always would, but in a different way. There were so many other beautiful things. I thought about my mother lying in the hospital thinking the baby was going to die, and yet worrying about us. Not wanting Poppa to feel the blame. Wanting me to know everything would be all right. And Poppa. He hadn't had a drink in over two months and he was going to meetings almost every night. And Mercedes. The baby, too. He didn't even have a name yet, just Baby Dohr. I thought he should be named Leonard. That means "strong as a lion," and that's what he was. The doctor said that every time he saw him. "This baby shouldn't be here. Never thought he'd make it." But he did.

I must have fallen asleep because the next thing I knew, Sarah was saying good night and Mercedes was asking me not to fall asleep again because we were almost home. And when we were, we tiptoed to the kitchen and made cocoa. Mercedes had told me she had something to tell me, but I already knew what it was. It was time for her to go.

We took the cocoa up to my room. Mercedes sat in

the rocker; I sat on the floor next to her. We sipped the cocoa and ate cookies just the way we'd done so many times before. When we were finished, she took something from her pocket and handed it to me. "This belongs to you," she said. It was the ring.

"But it's yours," I said.

"Not anymore."

I slipped it on my finger, knowing I'd never take it off.

Then we talked. She told me about New York and how different it is from Harmony. "Won't find a room like this up there," she said. She told me one last time about Elvis and Humes High. But this time it was different. All I could think of was that she'd had to leave there, too.

"Did anybody say good-bye on your last day?"

"I don't remember," she said. "It hurt so bad. Like no other hurt before or since. I was sent to the principal's office and he told me what I already knew. Humes High didn't allow Negroes. Then I had to go back and pack my things in the middle of the class. I was so desperate to leave that classroom before I cried, I just concentrated on how many steps it would take to get to the door."

She rocked for a bit and said, "The picture was one of the things I packed." She laughed a little. "Always thought I'd put it on the mantel of my settling-down place."

I felt like crying when she said that. But I didn't let myself.

"They weren't bad people, Wanda. It's just the way it was."

We didn't talk for a long while. And when she did, there were tears in her eyes. "It's been good being here," she said. "Real good." Then she looked down at me and said, "You think there's a mantel big enough for all forty-two of us?"

She laughed and so did I, and then we talked and talked, and when it was time to go to bed, I said, "I forgot to tell you something."

"What?"

"Sarah likes the Beatles now."

"They're a good group."

"She said they're better than Elvis."

"Really?"

"That's what she said."

"She's a traitor."

"Did you ever meet them?"

"Excuse me?" she said.

"Did you ever meet them?"

She looked at me, her eyes wide. The she stood up and laughed so hard she could barely get the words out. "No, I have never met them. Any of them. And no, I never went to school with them. I never had my picture taken with them. And I don't know what they do with their hair. And I don't care. And no, I do not want to meet them. So there."

I laughed, too, so hard and so long my face hurt. Tears streamed down Mercedes's cheeks and I couldn't tell whether they were from laughing or crying. When we finally stopped, I went over and took my quilt from my bed.

I didn't want to talk anymore so I just placed it in her arms and the two of us started downstairs. When we got to her room, she hugged me hard. She kissed me and said, "Don't you forget me, sweetie. And remember, we got to sparkle and shine in this life, you in your way, me in mine."

I held on to her and thanked her for coming to our house. I told her I loved her and that I'd never forget her. And then I said, "Please come back. Mr. Gingrich really loves you. And he said he'd wait forever."

She opened her door and turned to go in but looked back at me and whispered, "Nothing is forever." Then she smiled and touched my face. "Nothing at all. Not for any of us."